THE HIDDEN SIN

Volume 2
Truths & Betrayal

By
R.J. Levesque

The Hidden Sin V2:
Truths & Betrayal

©2011 R.J. Levesque

ISBN: 978-0-9867191-4-1

An RJL Publication

To my Mother, Father, Sister
And other Family and Friends

Previously on The Hidden Sin...

The town of Greensburg held a ceremony for their high school graduates. The valedictorian, Karen Hannah, had been missing for two weeks and her best friend, Carol Graham decided to take her place on the stage to perform the opening speech. But after a moment of darkness due to a power outage, Carol Graham had disappeared, leaving a black silhouette on the stage floor.

Jake Miller, graduate of Greensburg High School, had been living with his relatives Laura Chambers and his cousin Becky since the tragic, yet questionable suicide of his mother. He was visited by one of the deputies of the Greensburg Police Department and long-time friend Alan Craig to deliver Jake's diploma and told him that they had found Karen Hannah. She was found between her bedroom floor and the living room ceiling.

While Jake was having lunch with Alan and the deputy's sister Alice at the town's diner, they learned that Old Man Peterson had been peeping into Betty Schultz's bedroom window, which happened to be next door to Karen Hannah's house and may have been the last person that had seen the missing valedictorian.

After being attacked by an unknown, shadowy presence, Jake went to the police station to where Old Man Peterson was held for disturbing the peace. The town's pervert claimed he saw black figure grabbing Karen and pulling her to the bedroom floor.

Alice Craig learned, after receiving Karen's diary at her funeral by her parents, that the speech that the valedictorian had written also contains a confession that she had lied and cheated all of her school life and had the chemistry teacher, Dr. William Cummings involved. To confirm that, she had her deputy brother to retrieve the speech that was collected as evidence. The two siblings discovered that Karen and Cummings did a psychiatric session together due to the chemistry teacher's loss of his wife and a possibility some discrete activity also took place.

Alice agreed to tag along with Jake to sneak into the school, in which had turned into a crime scene due to possibility that Carol may show up dead just like Karen only to be caught by a patrolling officer.

Alan went to question the chemistry teacher about his involvement with the scandal but was then attacked and pulled into a nearby wall, through a dark, slimy pool, by several child-like hands. Faces of little girls appeared in that pool as it was later discovered that William Cummings was responsible for the reported ten missing little girls when Sheriff Clarence Barkley had found several child-size skeletons wearing dresses, buried in the Chemistry teacher's garden.

After being suspended from the police force by the disbelieving and sceptical Sheriff, Alan and Alice went to see Jason Baker about his accident in the woods near the Greensburg Campgrounds while arriving back from Carlton City, as Jake was held in a cell for interfering with the crime scene. Jason claimed he hit a moose hard enough that the motor would not start, which was why he could not make it to Karen Hannah's funeral.

After a close and secret inspection of the his dad's pick-up truck, it turned out that Jason had accidentally ran over a wondering child, hid the body in the woods, damages the pick-up to make it look like he hit a large animal and cut the ignition wires just to protect his opportunity that he had given to be a professional football player for Carlton City.

Alice tried to contact the police but her hulking boyfriend had threatened to kill her if the word is out. Alan jumped in to stop Jason, but gotten injured in the fight. But Jason's shadow suddenly came alive wearing the face of the toddler he had killed and pulled him into the darkness, but eventually lost an arm thanks to Alan's curiosity and the entity's weakness against direct light.

As Jake was resting in his cell, Old Man Peterson was snoring loudly in his cell next door to him. He then suddenly went silent. Moments later, Jake's shadow emerged from the concrete wall behind him and attempted to pull him in. But with his friends out of reach and the certainty that Old Man Peterson had been abducted as well, Jake shut his eyes tight and screamed.

Prologue

HE was halfway through. From his lower abdomen to his feet, Jake was moments away from being fully submerged under the black, deep-cold pool that manifested in his own shadow, on the back wall of his jail cell. The lower-half of his body had become numb and he held on to the framing of the suspended bed for dear life as the dark, oily entity was pulling him in.

There was no one to save him. Alan had lost his badge after telling the overly-strict sheriff of Greensburg about what happened to William Cummings and had no authority to unlock the jail cell. Old Man Peterson, held in his own cell next door to Jake, could have possibly been abducted before it reached its main target since he didn't react to any commotion that was going on. And finally, Jake's relatives, Aunt Laura Chambers and his nine-year-old cousin Becky, would not arrive at the station to pick him up until tomorrow.

Several thoughts had gone through Jake's mind while still attempting to hold on to his fragile and only life. The thoughts of whatever the outcome would be if he would be completely submerged. Would he end up like Karen Hannah, all bones and no flesh? Would he just disappear from the face of the Earth like Carol Graham? And if he would die, will he be able to see his mother and father again?

That thought stayed in Jake's mind. Meeting his parents again in heaven after losing them at the age of six would be something he looked forward to. The fun times they shared and away from all the bad things that had happened in the past. Though, he would not question about his mother's suicide if he did die. He just wanted to be with them again. And at that moment, for Jake, it did not sound like a bad idea.

One of the slimy, oily hands that were pulling him into the pool had reached up and grabbed onto his head. Jake was already losing his strength and felt his stomach and rib cage getting wet and already getting numb by the deep-cold temperature of the substance itself. The hand that gripped his head was just as cold and was trying to shake it off. No use, it latched onto him like an octopus.

This was it, he thought. Several more seconds and Jake would see his parents again. His thoughts kept running through his mind like videotape going fast-forward. The sounds were squeaky and swift like a talking chipmunk until it slowed down to particular scene in which he had remembered.

He remembered being in school, the hard rain, and seeing a tow truck hauling his mother's car waiting outside. The truck belonged to Derek Craig, Alan and Alice's father and Jake's mother was waiting in the passenger seat for her six-year-old son.

But what was more memorable about the whole scene, was after Jake climbed into the tow truck and rode off. His mother looked at his innocent-looking face with a glowing, loving smile. But one thing that Jake was sure of at that time; it was the last time his mother smiled at him.

VOLUME 2

TRUTHS & BETRAYAL

Chapter 1

THE skies were covered in gloomy, semi-dark layers of rain clouds. The heavy rain that fell from them hit the town of Greensburg like several angels crying from the heavens. To some people, that was what they thought. The heavens were crying for several unloved and wretched souls for nearly a few days and the people walking along the streets tried to hide from the huge tears. Several cars drove through the streets, splashing the rain onto the sidewalk as well as any unlucky soul in close proximity to them.

The town's diner was no different. The sound of the hard rain hitting on the roof was loud enough for the people inside to hear them. The atmosphere was gloomy as if they were tired and somewhat pissed off at Mother Nature. There was hardly any conversation going on but the music softly playing from an old jukebox had kept everyone at ease, except for a few short-tempered transport drivers, complaining about the cleanliness of their plates in which they were served with.

"What the hell is this?" one of them shouted. "I'm not eating that with a dirty plate! Get me a cleaner one!"

"I'm sorry, sir," Betty Schultz said as she took the dirty plate filled with chicken breasts and potatoes. "I'll get you a clean one right away."

Betty placed the dirty plate on the counter and called out the manager who also happened to be her husband.

"Not again," Ryan Schultz sighed as he walked quickly toward the back room of the diner. "Olivia!"

Olivia Chambers nearly jumped when she heard her name shouted like a mad dog. She nearly dropped a handful of utensils in which she was drying off.

"I got another complaint about them dirty dishes," Ryan yelled. "Smarten up, will you?"

"Sorry, Ryan," Olivia replied, a bit shaken. "I'll do better."

Ever since her husband, Detective Jeremy Miller of the Carlton City Police Department, was killed, things had gone downward. He had left his family with nothing. Not even any insurance to cover the funeral cost. Even though it was held by the Carlton City Police Department, they had only paid half of the cost and left the rest to the widow to take care of. Not only that, Jeremy also left with large amounts of debt. Three credit cards maxed out; even his line of credit attached to his bank account was nearly maxed out. And then there was the mortgage on the house both Olivia and her son Jake were living in after they moved out of the city. That mortgage was also under Jeremy's name.

Because of all these debts and funeral costs, Olivia had no choice but do two jobs to get the debts paid up and keeping a roof under her and her son. By day, she worked at the town's local diner owned by Ryan Schultz, and by night she worked at the local bar. Though, the bar was known to be very quiet except for the weekends, but between those two jobs and the hours they had both given her, she only had time to spend with her son Jake for almost two hours.

At least her sister Laura decided to watch over him during the evenings and Jake would sometimes visit his friend Alan after school to help each other out with their homework. Seeing those two in Olivia's eyes had always brought a smile on her face, as if Alan had suddenly become Jake's big brother. They would play outside, hid in Alain's tree house that he and his father Derek had built and would even sometimes walk to school and back along with Alan's little sister Alice. At least he would not feel alone with them around.

To make it worse, working two jobs tend to wear your body down after several weeks and having your depression take over as well. The loss of Olivia's husband was so terrible for her and Jake. It had already been a month since the funeral and she was having a difficult time coping with the loss. The memory of that dreadful phone call on their wedding anniversary to the rifle shots echoing through the sky at the funeral had burned into her mind and could not seem to shake it off and the thought of the financial troubles that her husband had left to his family.

All that had already begun to suck the life out of Olivia's body with each and every day that passed. And the only thing she could think of was some sort of miracle to lift all her troubles and sadness from her withering body and soul. Because the burden she had to carry was too much for her that she could not even hold a dinner plate in her hand from falling.

"Olivia!" Ryan shouted as he heard the dinner plate shattering into pieces.

The sound of the broken plate and the barking voice of Olivia's boss was more than enough for her to bear. All she could do after was running off into the break room at the back of the diner shedding tears. Both Betty and Ryan watched her go as Betty bit her lower lip, feeling sorry for what Olivia was going through.

Olivia sat in the break room crying over excessive exhaustion and fatigue. She only glanced at the nearby clock for a minute. It read 4:30pm. Her shift was already done and in the next two-and-a-half hours, her night shift at the local bar would start.

Betty walked in holding a slip of paper and sat next to Olivia with his right hand on her shoulder.

"You okay, Olivia?" Betty asked softly.

"I'm so sorry," Olivia replied. "I didn't mean to run off like that."

"Don't worry about it. Everyone has their share of problems."

"It's just that it's getting harder every time. I don't know if I can keep this up."

"I remember when you and little Jake first moved here and started working here. You were so full of life and energy that it reminded me of my mother when she was the manager of this diner. Every day you clock in and out, you always carry a smile on your face, just like her. Hell, I was around Jake's age at that time."

Olivia also remembered the day she and Jake moved into Greensburg. Her first thought of settling in was to look for a job and the first place she would go would be the diner. When she gave Ryan her application and told him the whole story about the reason Jeremy stayed in Carlton City and had not been divorced yet, Ryan hired her right away. He had told her that the people of Greensburg were always there to help each other out.

"But ever since Jeremy's funeral," Betty continued, "it was like your entire soul had been washed away along with that smile and energy. And it's affecting your job performance. I know losing your husband was a terrible loss for you. But you can't let that ruin your way of life."

"I'm trying, Betty." Olivia tried to say under her tears. "It's just that…" She shook her head. "He was a wonderful man and a good father to Jake. Why did it happen? Why did God took him away from us?"

Betty shook her head. "I don't think your husband's murder was God's will. Carlton City is a very violent city and I understood why you moved out of there. But the idea of Jeremy deciding to stay behind because of his job doesn't sound like an ideal man to me."

Betty slowly showed Olivia the slip of paper that she brought. "Here."

"What's this?" Olivia asked.

There was silence for a second and Betty replied with much regret. "Ryan told me to give you this. It's your last pay check. I'm sorry, dear."

Olivia's teary eyes widened and her heart somehow stopped for a second. She thought she would get her pay check on Fridays but since it was Wednesday, the amount printed on the check was not adequate enough for the week, not even for Olivia's eyes to accept.

"You're firing me?" Olivia said with somewhat shaken voice.

"Ryan said he can't keep you here with your depression messing up your job performance and your well being. You got to find a way clear that up and move on. Get a fresh start, get some help. You've got a son with you and he's all you have left. He's still six years old and has a huge future ahead of him. Don't let that go to waste because of your grief. Sure, you lost a husband and a caring father but you got to learn to move on."

"He would be considered caring if he hadn't chosen his job over his family." Olivia bluntly said, almost out of anger. After saying that, she suddenly got out of the chair, and slid a time card in an old fashioned punch machine.

Olivia just wanted to leave the diner and go straight home. But the skies were still crying heavily over the streets. The rain drops had turned the roads into very shallow rivers and every vehicle that passed by pushed the rain water aside. With her jacket and hood on, she was ready to climb into her car and drive to the school in which Jake was patiently waiting.

After climbing into the car, she inserted the key in the ignition and turned it. The sound of the starter was going on but the engine would not start. Olivia turned the ignition again and still, all she heard was the starting sound.

"Oh, please," Olivia said to herself. "Don't do this to me…"

First the complaints of the dirty dishes, then a broken dinner plate following by the loss of her job to an old car that wouldn't start. Olivia wanted to burst into more tears and almost felt like slamming her fists on the steering wheel. But all she could do, because she was weak and tired was to lay her head on the steering wheel bawling her eyes out.

There was a knock on the window of driver seat. The sounded nearly made Olivia jump.

"You alright, Olivia?" a familiar voice was barely heard but muffled by the window.

Olivia lowered down the window just for bit to see who the stranger was and to shield her from the rain falling into the car.

"Derek," Olivia said, feeling a bit relief of seeing an old friend. "Dear, God. I'm so glad to see you. My car wouldn't start."

"Yeah, I can see that. Mind if you could pop the hood open?"

Olivia pulled a small lever located underneath the steering wheel and close to the driver door. The hood popped up and Derek had already opened it to investigate the guts of the car. After a small moment Derek closed it back and walked back to the driver's side.

"You got a cracked distributor cap and all this rain is making your spark plugs and wires wet." Derek told Olivia. "Looks like you won't go anywhere until we get them replaced."

Olivia felt defeated and disappointed. "I was supposed to pick up Jake from school."

"Then why don't you hop in with me and we can pick him up now," Derek suggested. "I'll tow your car to my shop after and I'll be glad to give you a ride to the bar as well."

Olivia gave a smile of relief. "Thank you so much, Derek. But I don't think I have any money to pay you for the towing."

Derek winked. "Don't worry about it. Helping out a friend is more important than money."

Olivia climbed into Derek's tow truck as her next door neighbour in his early thirties, attached her car to a giant hook and lifted the front end a few feet in the air. Having a helping friend like Derek had always calmed her spirit. Even though she felt a bit sorry for him since he too used to live in Carlton City with his ex-wife. He had to leave her due to the excessive drinking she had gone through and a possibility of working as a prostitute.

He had told Olivia that living in a corrupt city like that may also have the ability to corrupt even the most innocent and clean soul, since Derek's ex-wife kind and loving woman to begin with. She would go to church every Sunday, pray every night, lending a helping hand to the needy and getting involved with several fund raisers and charities. But everything about her had changed during that faithless night when the scum of the city decided to soil her good spirit and faith.

It did not take long for Derek to receive a call from the Carlton City Police Department that his wife was raped and beaten to a near pulp. The assailants stole her purse, her money and her dignity all at the same time, and left her in an alley surrounded by foul garbage and waste. It completely changed her and her life ended up being a total wash-out. Drinking all the time and even started smoking. Hell, Alice was still in diapers and the mother acted like she didn't care anymore.

Seeing a completely different woman than the one Derek fell in love and married, it forced him to take his children and move out of the city to the small town of Greensburg in which it was considered to be peaceful and friendly. It was definitely the right choice for Derek, and it seemed like the right choice for Olivia to move out as well. But for her, it was completely different.

"Alright," Derek said to Olivia as he climbed onto the driver's seat. "We're all set."

Jake waited inside the school building on the other side of the main doors. There was so much rain falling that not even his yellow rain coat would keep him dry enough. But that did not stop him from singing his favourite raining song to pass the time.

Jake saw a tow truck stopping on the side of the curb and noticing his mother's car attached behind it. He recognized the truck right away and pushed the doors open with a happy smile. He quickly put up his yellow hood and raced down the walkway across the heavy rainfall as the passenger door slowly swung open. His mother was waiting for him in the passenger seat.

"Hurry, Jake," Olivia called out to her son. "You don't want to get too wet."

Jake made it inside the truck. "Whew," he sighed. "That's a lot of rain."

"Put your seatbelt on, honey." Olivia told him.

Jake did just that.

"What's up big guy?" Derek said to little Jake.

"Hello, Mr. Derek," the innocent looking child replied. "Alan didn't come to school today."

"I know. He just got a nasty cold, thanks to the weather we're having."

"Oh that's too bad," Olivia said. "Well, I hope he gets better soon."

Derek glanced at Jake. "Well, maybe you can cheer him a bit since we're dropping you two off at my place so I can fix your mom's car."

"That sounds like a good idea," Olivia nodded. "Just don't get too close, or you'll get sick too."

"Does that mean I have to hold my breath?" Jake asked with a bit of curiosity.

Both Derek and Olivia laughed at the child's suggestion.

"You can try," Olivia said. "But I don't think that's how the common cold works."

The time all three had spent together inside the tow truck brought a bit of hope into Olivia's soul. Perhaps Betty was right. She would need to find away to start over and get a fresh start. Not just for her sake but for the sake of her only son. She cannot sit and cry all day and night. She would have to put all that behind her and move forward with her life as well as Jake's. But one thing was for certain; by the time Jake would grow up, she would tell him something that had kept hidden from him ever since she and Jeremy brought their son into the world. But until then, she would have to concentrate on what was lying ahead for them. Of course, there were some financial obstacles to overcome, but money is only an object. What was more important was the well being of her six-year-old boy and the love and care she had given him. With both of them sharing a warm smile in their faces, a certain thought had gone through her mind, in which she knew, even if she would have told Jake the real truth of his existence, would be a complete and total lie.

Everything will be fine.

*****

Every time Jake remembers that smile, it almost shed made him shed a tear. Since it was the last time she ever smiled at him, it was something memorable and something he would keep in his memories until the last breath of his existence seep out of his lungs. With his entire body excluding his head and left arm, still holding onto the framing of the suspended bed, fully submerged into the black pool, he would want to see his mother's smile once more. No, not just his mother, but both her and his father at the same time.

He would call out to them the minute he would see them on the other side. But for some reason, he could not utter a single word. Just gargles and choking sounds were spewing out of his lungs as the black slimy substance found its way into his throat. It did not taste good at all. It was like tasting death itself, like something cold and rotten that was kept in the refrigerator for too long. It was so revolting that you would choke to death before it could fill up your lungs and drown you.

Jake did not want to end his life that way. There were still some unanswered questions regarding his mother's suicide and the memory loss he had suffered. But seeing as he was minutes, or maybe even seconds to be completely devoured by this supernatural monster, it looked like it didn't matter if he had gotten the answers or not. At that moment, he just wanted to let it all go. And with that in mind, Jake released his grip from the bed framing.

"Hold on, Jake!" a familiar voice cried out. "I got you!"

Strong, firm hand gripped on to Jake's left arm. It was Alan and the deputy that was napping at the desk nearby.

"Help me, damn it!" Alan yelled at the deputy. "I've only got one arm working, here!"

Of course, Alan was only able to reach out with his left hand since his right hand tucked away at his side, due to the broken bones of his right arm thanks to his sister's overprotected, sports fanatic boyfriend Jason Baker.

Alan and the deputy pulled Jake with all their might, but it appeared to be difficult as there was some powerful force behind the black pool that was holding him back. It was like pulling someone out of a tar pit opposed to saving a person from drowning in quicksand or freezing water after falling through the ice. Even with several huge tugs and grunts, they were only able to pull Jake a few inches at a time and possibly another two inches a minute after.

Alan suddenly thought that his strength and the young deputy's would be completely exhausted before they can liberate Alan's childhood friend from the cold, dark horror. But with a certain spark in his mind, the suspended Greensburg Police officer had an idea, in which he would also consider it risky.

"Deputy," Alan called out to his helper. "Grab my flashlight."

The deputy had no idea what he meant by it but he did what he was told. He grabbed Alan's flashlight attached to his belt strap. "On three, I want you to shine some light on all that black shit!"

The deputy pointed the torch at the wall of black bile as he watched it swimming and swirling on the concrete wall. He was already shaking in his boots the minute he saw Jake's head sticking out of the wall like as if he was being swallowed by it. Though, he had already gotten used to it, since he was the one who found Karen Hannah's body underneath the missing valedictorian's bedroom.

"One," Alan counted as the deputy gripped the flashlight tightly in his left hand and Jake's arm in right. "Two," the deputy's left thumb laid onto the black switch of the flashlight. "THREE!"

And with a click of the switch, a burst of Heaven's light burst from the circular base of the flashlight and engulfed the black horror with its glory. The effect was instant as shrieks, cries, and convulsions erupted from the black pool as the creature felt the burning pain of light.

The powerful force that held Jake had suddenly dissipated and both Alan and the deputy were able to pull him out of the pool in an instant. Though Alan knew that if they hadn't pulled him out the second the light hit the creature, it would start burning away and it would have eaten through Jake's flesh within seconds, similar to what had happened with Jason Baker.

The black pool had somehow hardened itself and became a black stain on the concrete wall of the jail cell as Jake was lying on the floor, covered in the same black bile that was all over Karen Hannah's remains, and shaking uncontrollably due to the super cold temperature. His whole body was numb, and he was slowly going into shock.

"Jake," Alan called out to his friend, trying to get a response by shaking him. But the black bile was so cold to the touch that just by touching his shoulder, his palm almost went numb. "You okay, buddy?"

"I've already called the ambulance," the deputy said to Alan.

"What about Old Man Peterson?"

"He's dead. He probably had a heart attack while he was sleeping."

Alan turned back toward his shaken friend for a second then returned his gaze to the deputy. "Get a blanket or something," he said, "until the ambulance arrives."

The deputy went off to find one as Alan tends to his friend.

Why Jake? Alan thought. Why is this thing after him?

Chapter 2

JAKE felt a slight soreness in his left cheek. His eyes opened but he could only see the night light coming from the hallway, outside his bedroom door. He wasn't sure if it was the soreness of his cheek that woke him, or the urge to go to the bathroom. Either way, he had to get out of the bed before he wets it again. Even though he noticed a small stain of blood on his pillow, he would not waste any time to figure out where that came from.

Just outside the bedroom and into the hallway, the bathroom was just across. Luckily, the house had two bathrooms, so the idea of just running down the stairs and turn right would be a waste of time, and Jake would not had made it there without wetting his new pyjamas that his mother had bought him.

Jake was just about to step in until he suddenly heard a noise. A creaking noise, similar to what you would hear from an old rocking chair, but it didn't sound like the creaking noise of wooden object. It sounded almost metallic, like the turning of a knob when closing a water faucet, but more lower pitched, like as if it was something heavy.

The hallway was dark by the night and there was barely some light shining through the window at the far end and from a street lamp outside the house. The path was barely visible but Jake knew where that hallway would lead.

Following the creaking noise, Jake slowly crept across the hallway, trying not to make any noise, in hoping he won't wake up his mother. The light revealing the pathway also showed that it would turn to the left, towards his mother's bedroom. That was where the noise came from, but he wasn't so sure if he wanted to go in and check it out. His mother could still be awake, and the sound could have been something that she may be doing.

Jake stopped right at the left turn of the hallway. His mind suddenly flickered like something had woken up in him, like a memory of some sort. Has he been there before?

"This feels familiar," Jake said to himself. But what surprised him was his voice. It did not sound like the voice of a six-year-old boy. It was his current, sixteen-year-old voice. And to make matters worse, he noticed his hands were not small, child-like hands.

I know where this is going, Jake thought. And above all else, he did not want to continue. He knew that if he walked into his mother's bedroom, he would see her lifeless body hanging by the neck and creaking noise was the sound of the little ceiling lamp, holding on to her weight. He did not want to experience that again, so he decided to turn back, heading back toward the bathroom.

Within an instant, the pathway behind him had suddenly changed into his mother bedroom with the ceiling lamp visible and little light coming from a lamp near his mother's bed.

What the hell is going on? Jake thought, as he stood in the doorway of his mother's bedroom. But his eyes widened with a bit of fear as he saw a familiar figure hanging by the ceiling lamp.

Tied to the ceiling lamp with an old, yellow rope, the noose end held the neck of Olivia Chambers Miller. Her fire-coloured hair was wet, as if she had been outside in the rain, which was strange because it wasn't raining that night. Her cold, blue eyes staring into nothingness and dried traces of tears on her cheeks were visible, like as she had cried before taking her own life.

"Mommy," Jake called out, except it was his six-year-old voice, not his current voice.

There was no response, but Jake already knew that. This was around the time where he saw his mother's body and fell unconscious but he was fully conscious, this time around. All he could think of was to run out of the bedroom and pretend that he had never saw it the second time.

The bedroom door suddenly slammed itself shut, preventing Jake from ever leaving. He tried to turn the doorknob but it would not budge. The keyhole underneath the knob suddenly began to fill and bleed thick, black liquid from its gaping hole and just barely touched the tip of his left big toe.

Jake felt an instant cold from that and quickly jumped away from the door. The black liquid began pouring out through the cracks and hinges of the door as Jake slowly stepped back, afraid and confused what was happening around him.

"*I'm sorry,*" a loud whisper echoed Jake's ears. "*I'm so sorry.*"

Jake turned toward the whisper. Olivia's dead eyes were somehow fixated on Jake. Her dried lips were barely seen, opening and closing, trying to mouth out the words.

"*I'm sorry,*" Olivia's cold and dead human shell repeated.

But because his mother was somehow speaking to Jake, he suddenly had the urge to eagerly ask her something.

"Why did you take your own life, mom?" Jake asked the cadaver "You're not the type of person who would do that and leave me at a young age. Why, mom? Why?"

Olivia's dead face had suddenly transformed into a flash of anger.

"*I hate you, and I wish you were dead!*" a child's voice erupted from her mother's mouth.

Jake recognized the child voice, but he could not understand the context of the words at all.

"*I hate you, and I wish you were dead!*" the body repeated loudly.

"That wasn't me," Jake shook his head. "I did not say that, Hell, I don't even remember saying that!"

"*I hate you, and I wish you were dead!*"

The words kept repeating over and over, trying to get into Jake's head. He wanted all this to end so he turned back towards the bleeding door. Only this time, the black liquid disappeared and Jake's very own shadow was visible on the surface of the wooden door. It stood there, and had not mimicked Jake's sudden movements all. It was breathing, living, like a real human being, but it looked menacing; as if it was the soul of a serial killer waiting to pounce onto his next victim. Yellow eyes were suddenly seen and the shadow hands emerged from the surface of the door and gripped Jake's neck like a pair of tentacles.

The shadowy figured pulled Jake closer to its dark and hidden visage, close enough to be nearly touching the tip of his nose.

"*Soon,*" a whisper seeped out of the shadowy figure, "*there will be no such thing as sin.*"

*****

Jake was already sitting up, drenched in sweat and breathing heavily. It was only a nightmare, he thought, and a really scary one at that. It was far worse than the original nightmare of his mother's suicide. But it had that shadowy demon, the black bile and finally some disembodied voices.

Jake looked around and noticed he was in a hospital room. Though he had no idea how he got here. All he remembered was being annoyed by Old Man Peterson's loud snoring and his own shadow pulling him into the wall. But all of his friends were out of his reach, so who could have possibly saved him? But Jake decided to lie back down, resting his head on the half-wet pillow, thanks to his sweat and ponder about the nightmare. Did Jake really say those words to his mother? And what did that shadow meant about having no such thing as sin?

A nurse walked into the room, almost running. After she heard the scream coming from Jake's room from the nearby desk, she had to find out what had happened.

"Are you alright, Jake?" the nurse asked worryingly.

"Yeah," Jake replied to the beautiful Asian nurse. "I just had a nightmare.

Nurse Sakura Yoshiro sighed in relief and gave Jake a gentle smile. Of all the nurses that worked at the Greensburg General Hospital, in Jake's opinion, Susie was the prettiest. Maybe it was due to the fact that Jake had a secret fondness of oriental women, especially the ones from Japan. Sakura Yoshiro had been in Canada for only two years and she had been a nurse in Greensburg's town hospital for nearly five months. Her move to Canada was due to her father's job transfer after she finished her course in medicine at the Tokyo University. At least by studying in Canada, she was aiming to become a full fledged doctor. And for her being a nurse was a good start in order to understand how to take care of patients and examine any troubles with that may occur.

Jake returned the smile back at the twenty-four-year-old nurse. Just seeing her smile made him wonder if any of the male patients, especially the elderly, had ever woken up to see a pretty face like Sakura's. And he was pretty sure that Amanda Riley, Becky's best friend and dying from a serious illness, whenever she would open her eyes, she would see the face of an angel.

Jake's mind sparked some curiosity about his own whereabouts. "How did I get here, anyways?" he asked Sakura.

"Alan brought you here," Sakura replied while going through the clipboard. "You both came in the same ambulance."

That's impossible, Jake thought. How could he had known what was happening in his jail cell?

"Where is he now?"

"He's being treated for a broken arm. I'll let him know that you're awake."

After jotting down some notes, Sakura grabbed blood pressure strap and wrapped around Jake's arm.

"How is Amanda doing, anyways?" Jake asked.

The nurse shook her head. A hint of sadness was easily seen in her expression, indicating that Amanda had not have a lot of time left in this world. Seeing the nurse's answer, Jake started thinking about Becky and how she was going through as her best friend was very close to passing away in to Heaven, and how it will affect her life in her coming years.

Jake also felt sorry for Amanda's parents, since they didn't have enough money to send her to Carlton City and being operated by specialists. I'm mean, sure. Her parents have medical insurance for something like that, but that was only valid in Greensburg. The medical insurance policy in Carlton City is completely different, ever since the new mayor arrived. And no one is able to understand why the prime minister of Canada wouldn't do anything to fix it and make it as equal as the rest of the provinces. And because of the different policies, Amanda's parents would have to pay the fee for the surgery in which they could not afford. The entire town of Greensburg, including the mayor, had even donated some money to help out. But those greedy sons of bitches demanded more. And with that, the entire town felt that all of their efforts to help Amanda were in vain.

"You're finally awake," Alan said as he walked into the room, wearing a sling and a right arm wrapped in a cast.

"What happened to you?" Jake asked.

"Jason Baker. Alice and I found out that he was the one who ran over and killed that toddler in the woods near the Greensburg Campgrounds on his way back from Carlton City. He was threatening her to keep that from the police, just to protect his only chance of being a player for the city's football team."

"I thought he hit a moose. I walked by his house when I was going to the diner to have lunch with you guys. His dad's pick-up was in pretty bad shape."

"He made it look like he hit a moose. A couple of witnesses heard a crash. The pick-up ran into a tree, Jason went out and did more damage before driving off. And as for the story of the motor not working, he had the ignition wires cut after arriving home. When Alice went for her cell phone, Jason nearly tried to kill her."

Jake could not believe what he heard. He then shook his head with disbelief. He never thought that Jason would kill his own girlfriend to prevent any word of the accident to the police and lose his chance of obtaining his dream. I mean, there are some people who are huge fanatics and wanted to make a name for them, but to cover up a mistake that may hamper your dreams would make thing even worse in the long run. And Jason did not believed in learning from your mistakes. Only two things he believed in and those were winning and the rewards for winning.

"What happened to Jason after that?" Jake asked, looking back at Alan.

"He's gone," Alan sighed. "Disappeared, just like what happened to William Cummings. And just like the others, he left a silhouette of himself on the wall."

This is fucking crazy, Jake thought. Four people abducted, one of them dead and another missing an arm, and all of them left a shadow print of themselves. There had to be some sort of significance to why those prints were left behind. But Jake suddenly decided to stop thinking about it, as the thought of Alice suddenly struck his mind.

"Where is Alice, anyway?" Jake asked.

"I took her home last night and came here to get my arm fixed," Alan replied. "They let me sleep here for the night, since it was very late. She told me she was going to the church in the morning to pray. The poor girl was shocked out of her mind when she saw Jason's lost arm lying on her lap like that."

"I don't blame her. Seeing a severed arm in real life and in the movies are totally different things."

Jake remembered the horror movies he had seen in the past that involved dismemberment. Despite some of their shock value, they did not make him squirm. Although Alice was the exact opposite, one look of someone being decapitated on the movie screen and she immediately looked away in disgust. But having a real arm falling on her lap was way too much for her, not to mention that it belonged to her boyfriend.

Alan sat at the foot of the bed with so much thought.

"I'm starting to think that these abductions have something in common." Alan said.

Jake began to run the past events in his mind and suddenly realized what Alan meant. "Come to think of it," he said, "each of those abductees did something bad in their lives."

"Karen Hannah and Carol Graham both cheated their way through school in order to get accepted at the Carlton City University to become psychiatrists. William Cummings was responsible for kidnapping, molesting and killing those ten missing girls, and Jason ran over a little child in the woods, hid the body and damaged his father's pick-up to look like he hit a moose just to protect his chance of being a pro football player."

Thinking about all those incidents had made Jake thought about his experience with this shadow creature, how he got the bruises around his neck in which Alan was able to see from where he was sitting, and that time when he was in jail.

"Whatever this thing is," Alan continued, "If this keeps up, it may go after everyone in town."

"Anybody who committed a sin," Jake said to himself, recalling the recent nightmare he had and the whispering voice he heard from the shadowy demon. "And soon, there will be no such thing as sin."

"What was that?" Alan could not grasp what his friend had said. But Jake decided to keep whatever thoughts about the nightmare to himself and shook his head.

"But what I want to know is why this thing is after me," Jake added. "I mean, have I ever done anything wrong?

Alan shrugged a little. "I don't know either. As long as I have known you, you haven't done anything wrong. Sure, we made few bad things in the past but that's just kids stuff."

Jake did remember some of the shenanigans he and Alan had pulled when they were kids. One of the worst was when they snuck into Old

Man Peterson's house and stole some of his skin magazines. Of course, Peterson wasn't that old at the time, but he was still one of Greensburg's worst citizens. He would eventually have caught them both, but they had been eluding from capture for a good while, until Sheriff Barkley received a call from Peterson.

Alan stood up from the bed with a sense courage and sincerity. "Well, if I were you, I wouldn't wrap my head around it right now. You should rest up a bit. And don't worry about a thing. Cop or no cop, I still I got your back, Jake."

Seeing Alan's encouraging smile had acknowledged Jake he would stand by his word. But hearing them made Jake almost bit his lip. Hearing those words felt like a reminder of something that he had not told Alan, something he had hidden from his best friend for a long time.

That day when Alan got accepted at the Police Academy in Carlton City would made Jake proud, but when he finally earned his badge and saluted, the real feeling of being proud was not among him. Just a feeling of regret and the decision Jake had made to keep his involvement of his friend's triumph a secret would make him regret even more. If he were to tell Alan about his involvement, it would cost Jake terribly, more likely a supportive and long-time friend of Greensburg.

Two familiar people walked into the room as Jake noticed the shortest one was carrying a small bouquet of flowers.

"Hey there, big guy," Aunt Laura said as little Becky nearly ran into her big cousin with opened arms.

Both Becky and Jake shared each other a hug, but for a small girl, she nearly had enough strength to squeeze the life out of him.

"Careful, Becky," Alan said laughing a little. "Keep this up and your cousin may end up using an oxygen tank."

Becky gave Jake a worried but mean look. "That's twice that you've been sent here. You know what happens in baseball, right?"

Jake nodded with a laugh. Yeah, he thought. Three strikes and your out, but in this case it would be three strikes and your dead.

"How are you feeling?" Jake's aunt asked.

"A little stiff," Jake replied. "But I do feel a bit of numbness in my toes."

"I bet," Alan said. "That back stuff you were covered with so damn cold to the touch."

"What black stuff?" Laura asked, giving the curious look to Alan.

"He was covered in that same black substance that was found all over Karen Hannah's remains. He was very lucky that I came back to the police station in time after that fiasco with Jason Baker."

Laura's eyes widened, as if a flashback of a certain memory that was stored at the very back of her mind was struck so hard that it ended up in the front. Whatever that memory was, it made her bit her lower lip. What made it worse was Jake saw her reaction, as if she may had seen the black bile before.

"You've seen it before, Aunt Laura?" Jake asked curiously.

Laura shook her head, trying to avoid the question.

"Well," Alan added, "all that matters is that you're still alive."

Jake smiled to Alan again, feeling grateful for his best friend and his heroic deed. He could not imagine what would happen if that shadowy being would have taken him completely. But he decided not to think about it and turned his sights on his little cousin.

"How about we go visit Amanda?" Jakes asked her.

"Okay," the pigtailed nine-year-old girl replied softly.

"Are you sure it's okay for you to get out of bed?" Alan asked, being the big brother to his best friend.

"It's alright. I may be a bit stiff, but I got to move somehow. Besides, when was the last time you saw me this lazy?"

"Everyday after school," Becky teased.

Everyone in the room laughed as they walked out of Jake's recovery room and heading toward Amanda Riley's. They walked by several recovery rooms that housed several patients. A few sick people, a couple of children, but mostly elderly souls hanging by a thread, holding onto whatever strength they had left until the time of their passing. Seeing them like that reminded Jake about little eight-year-old Amanda Riley's condition and the very limited amount of time she had left to live.

Jake, Alan, Laura and Becky stopped at one particular room in which the sick and dying Amanda Riley lied still in the hospital bed with an oxygen mask on her pale face. The blond, pale eight-year-old friend of Becky Chambers was breathing silently as every ounce of her spirit slowly seeped away from her frail body with every exhale. She looked like a lifeless doll, waiting to be picked up and be loved again. Unfortunately, it looked like the only person who would pick her up and love her again would be God himself.

"Amanda?" Becky called out silently.

The sleepy blue eyes were revealed as her pale eye lids began to lift from their resting place. Amanda was able to see Becky standing next to her bed with a caring but sad smile. Her small, frail, right hand slowly lifted, reaching out to her best friend. Becky quickly took her hand a tear began to run down from her left eye, rolling down on her rosy cheek and landing on the bed sheet.

"Becky…" the little girl's voice was barely audible.

"This is my cousin Jake," Becky introduced.

Amanda's eyes slowly shifted to the tall teenager standing at the foot of the bed between Becky's mother and her cousin's friend. Her left hand raised a little, attempting to wave at Jake.

"Hi, Amanda," Jake said as he waved back at her. "It's nice to meet you."

Amanda slowly smiled and shifted her weakening gaze back to Becky. "You told me your cousin is cute."

Jake barely blushed. That reminded him the time when he was in middle school. He would sometimes notice a couple of girls glancing at him and whispering their thoughts to each other. Though he wasn't sure if they were saying he was good looking or looked like a total weirdo. But when he came across Alice Craig, she did not say any of those since they know each other as long as her brother had. Despite the fact that she was dating the school's sports jock and bully, Jason Baker, she did showed signs of fondness toward Jake. Maybe it was because she felt sorry for him to have lost both his parents at such a young age.

But Jake was a bit shy toward girls, even toward Alice. But with her boyfriend Jason Baker lurking in the shadows and keeping his eyes on him like a hawk, Jake decided not to get too close to Alice without risking getting beaten up or his faced shoved in the toilet.

Those memories were good to have as much as the memories of his parents. And Becky's memories of the fun times she had with Amanda would be something she would cherish. But both Jake and his aunt Laura could not imagine what impact it may do to Becky's life. She and Amanda had been very close, close enough to be sisters. The bond of friendship they had shared had never faltered over the years that they have known each other and the time they had spent. They never fought, never argued and never left each other's side. But having one of them dying right next to the other would have felt even worse that just having one moving out of the country. Everyone in town felt sorry for Amanda's parents and had already gave them their condolences but both Jake and Laura felt sorrier for Becky.

There was a silent knock at the door. Doctor Chandler's face slowly poked into the room.

"Excuse me," Jake's family doctor said. "I'm sorry if I'm interrupting anything. Jake, could I have a moment with you?"

"Okay," Jake replied and turned briefly toward Alan and Laura. "I'll be back in a bit."

Both Jake and Chandler stood outside of Amanda's room.

"How are you feeling, Jake?" Chandler asked.

"I'm doing fine," Jake replied rolling his shoulders a little. "Still a little stiff but I can still move."

"I'm glad to hear that." Chandler's face went from glad to a concerned look. "Jake, the substance that you were covered with, we took a sample of it we're running some tests to figure out its properties. But it's no doubt that it's the same stuff that was found at Karen Hannah's bedroom."

Jake nodded. "At least we get to know what it's made of and where it's coming from."

"But when I saw you came in covered in that, it sort of reminded me of the time when your aunt brought you hear unconscious, after your mother's death. I had to be certain it was just a coincidence so I had to pull out your old medical file from ten years ago."

"What's so special about it?" Jake asked a bit curious about what Chandler was talking about. "I had a traumatic shock of seeing her hung by the neck in her bedroom and fell unconscious. That's what you and Aunt Laura told me, right?"

There was small silence. Chandler had an old folder tucked in his right arm in which he showed to Jake. He felt a huge surge of regret, like as if there was more to it than just post-traumatic shock and he felt guilty of not telling him completely.

Jake grabbed the folder and opened it. In it was file date ten years ago with his name, age, gender and any physical statistic written on it. Below that looked like a summary what Chandler had witnessed when Jake was brought in after he fell unconscious.

Patient was brought in unconscious around twelve-thirty AM. His relative stated that he may have fell unconscious due to shock of seeing his mother's dead body. The relative had to be sent to the next room to be treated for what it looked like freezer burns on both her forearms. The freezer burns may come from this black substance in which this child was covered with.

After a quick examination, we've found that the black liquid had completely filled his lungs but did not understand how he could still be breathing as if any type of fluid that would fill a person's lungs to the top would eventually drown the victim.

After successfully cleaning out his entire system, the child regained consciousness the morning after but had no recollection of what had happened last night. He seemed to have lost some memory either due to the shock or something to do with the black substance. I will keep monitoring his condition and will provide any updates as they become available.

As for the black substance, I had the liberty of obtaining a sample and send it to the science labs in Carlton City. The reports came back saying it was pure crude oil, but being so deeply cold to the touch and how the patient was able to breathe with that in his lungs his still a mystery. Still, I decided to keep the information about the black substance to myself and to the relative who brought the child in, as it may cause pointless questions and probably more panic than it already has due to suicide of this child's mother.

I decided to help the child regain some of his memory and keep a close eye of any developments.

Jake's eyes widened and could not believe what he had read from Chandler's report. Both his doctor and his aunt had kept something very important from him for ten years. In other words, that time in Jake's bedroom, after Karen Hannah's funeral, when the shadowy demon attacked him, it wasn't really the first time. It was quite possible that this thing had attacked him in his mother's bedroom ten years ago, in which sort of cleared up what the nightmare Jake had recently with that creepy, whispering voice.

Jake felt disappointed, but felt a bit angry about it that he nearly dropped the file to the hospital floor. "Why didn't you tell me before?" Jake's voice rose slightly.

"You were too young to understand any of it," Chandler replied with a bit of sympathy and hoping he could forgive Jake for keeping that secret from him. "And with all of these disappearances that are happening around town and a possible link to what happened ten years ago, I had no other choice."

Jake slowly nodded angrily. "Yeah, you had a choice. You could at least let me die."

Jake angrily started walking away, heading back to his room. How could they have kept that from him? That shadow demon was around town even way before Karen Hannah was killed and nobody noticed? And if that thing had been around the time Jake's mother committed suicide, then she may have seen it too.

Jake arrived at his room and sat heavily on the bed, feeling angry and disappointed. He just wanted to smack the doctor's face in and burn that medical file like the whole talk about him and the black shit from ten years ago. He just wanted everything to be back to way it was. He fell unconscious by traumatic shock of seeing his mother's dead body hung on a ceiling lamp in her bedroom, period. No, living shadows, no anomalies, none of this bullshit about having no such thing as sin, nothing.

But Jake could not help that the abductions that occurred in town and what happened to him ten years ago along with his mother's suicide had some kind of relation to one another. More questions kept piling up as he was asking for answers, but all it ever did was making him so pissed off that he kind of wished all of this was just a big fat lie. He wondered what had exactly happened that night when he saw his mother's body, and why did she took her own life. And what about those voices he heard in that nightmare? The screaming, angry voice of a child disguised as Jake's own six-year-old-self and the eerie whisper of that dark entity. What could they possibly mean?

At a corner of his eye, there was tall, dark figure standing in front of the nurses' desk in which Jake was able to see from his room. It was difficult to see the man's face since he was wearing a huge trench coat, and dark glasses which pretty much concealed his identity. His hair was fine but very grey, like a man in his sixties or seventies. Something about that man looked familiar to Jake, he left as soon as he arrived.

Nurse Sakura walked into the room holding a small envelope. "Some man came and told me to give you this."

"Do you have any idea who it was?" Jake asked curiously.

The nurse shook her head. "No. It's hard to tell with those big, dark glasses he was wearing."

"Well, thanks anyway."

As soon as Sakura walked back out of the room, Jake took a small glance at the envelope. The name 'Jake' was written in big capital letters across the sheer white envelope. There was also no indication to whom it was from, in which it could possibly be written in the letter itself. But Jake did not hesitate to open the envelope as the inside of it was clearly a letter addressing to him.

'Dear Jake

I've came a long way to find you and I know that by now, certain things have been happening around the town of Greensburg and you had begun to question your past. I know what happened to you ten years ago and I would be happy to give you any answers that could possibly give you. But first, we need to meet up in person

We should meet up at the old house in which you and your mother had lived because a portion of your questions will be answered in there. Your mother had hidden something in the house in which no one was able to find after your mother's funeral. I'm not sure what it is either but she told me if something like this would have happened, she would give it to me or you.

We should meet up there around midnight and bring a flashlight, in case that thing comes out of your shadow again. It is very vulnerable against any direct light. But I advise you to come alone, since bringing someone else may compromise my cover.

Remember, bring a flashlight and come alone at your mother's house around midnight tonight. We will meet then.'

Answers to Jake's questions? Could he really be trusted? And what does this man could possibly want, Jake thought.

Chapter 3

THE morning sunlight had made its way through the stained glass windows of the church. Each window depicted a colourful image, representing the life of and death of Jesus Christ. The bright light from the song was strong enough that the colours on those windows could barely be seen on the varnished, wooden floor.

Alice was there, kneeling on small stool at the front bench on the right side. Her heart had never felt so hurt and filled with this much hope before. She was praying from her very pained heart and soul not just for the safety of Jason Baker, but the safety of others who had been snatched away from this world. She had prayed for hours and her knees were already sore due to the uncomfortable kneeling stools, but her prayers were more important than the slight pain she was getting.

Emerging from a small office behind the giant golden crucifix of Christ, Pastor Brian Mayne noticed Alice praying at the front bench.

"Oh, Alice," he said. "I didn't hear you come in."

Alice looked up and saw Mayne holding a brass goblet. She then suddenly noticed that Mayne's right side of his face was redder than the other side. It looked a bit like a sun burn of some sort.

"What happened to your face?" Alice asked.

The old priest nearly stuttered, trying to avoid the embarrassing question, like as if he was trying to hide it. "Oh, I was making some tea when a stray cat came out of nowhere and tripped over it. I had the kettle in my hand and the hot water went all over my face as I fell."

"How did you get a cat in here?"

"I may have left a window open at home. The weather outside was so nice that I may have opened it to let the fresh air in."

Mayne opened a small squared cabinet and stored the brass goblet away.

"How about some coffee, Alice?" the old priest asked. "Since I know you're not a tea drinker."

Alice got up from the bench. "Thank you, Father. I didn't get much sleep since what happened to Jason last night."

"Yes, I've heard about it. Let's talk about it in the office."

Alice walked into Mayne little office at the back of the church. The interior was very plain with white walls and an old, brown desk and a small filing cabinet at a nearby corner. There was also a painting of gorgeous scenery of green fields etched up on the back wall behind above the desk. According to what Mayne had told Alice, there was also a safe hid behind the painting in which all the donations that the church had collected were stored.

At the opposite side of the office, from the desk and the painting, there was a small sink with a tea kettle and a coffee maker, already filling up the pot with its black magic and two cups sitting next to it. Though seeing the coffee liquid dripping down into the pot reminded her of that monster that took Jason away and the destroyed visage of the little boy, whom Jason had killed, covered in that dark liquid.

Alice sat at the front of the desk as Pastor Mayne gave her a filled cup.

"Thank you," she said kindly.

Mayne sat down at his desk and took a few sips of the coffee. He noticed that Alice was staring into space for a moment and had a blank expression as if her mind was trying to clear up all that was going on.

"Is everything alright Alice?" Mayne asked.

"Do you think," Alice paused for a second. "Do you think that all of this is an act of God?"

"What do you mean?"

"I mean all those people who disappeared, they had done bad things. They've been taken away because of the terrible sins they've committed."

Mayne sighed. "I seriously don't think that this is an act of God, Alice. People do commit sins but they have the choice of atonement. That's why we have Sunday mass."

"But what about the ones who decided to lock their sin deep into their souls and tried to either forget or keeping it a secret, like William Cummings or Jason?"

Mayne took another sip of his coffee and leaned onto his desk with his arms rested firmly on the huge times table glued to it. "Alice, everyone has a hidden sin within our souls. Even such small ones can be long forgotten but still hidden within. Even I myself tend to lie or even curse the Lord's name in vain. Of course I always pray for his forgiveness afterwards."

Alice's thoughts suddenly shifted to that creature that had taken her boyfriend. "What about this...thing, this shadow thingy? Do you think it's after people who violate the Ten Commandments?"

Mayne gave some thought but then slowly nodded with somewhat uncertainty. "I'm not sure about that. If it's going after people who broke the Ten Commandments, then the whole town would have vanished by now, since almost everyone here may had broken the 'Though shall not lie' Commandment."

Pastor Mayne had a point. That thing would have abducted the entire town population if it would go after anyone who had broken the Ninth Commandments.

"But that commandment is actually a shorter, simpler term than the traditional interpretation, 'Though shalt not bear false witness against thy neighbour.'" Mayne added. "So I don't think that this creature would go after anyone who commits a mild fib."

Alice took a sip of her coffee. "If it's not going after the town, then it could mean that this thing is targeting its victims selectively."

Alice had a sudden thought that it may be just a coincidence and at the same time silly, but she needed to have a second opinion on what she had in mind. "Do you think that it would be possible," Alice said with a half-pause, "that someone may be controlling the thing?"

Pastor Brian Mayne gave curious look to what Alice had said. "What do you mean?"

"Like, I know this may sound a little bit silly, but in our History class, were discussing the Greensburg legend of the Black Cave, or it was also called, The Cave of Conviction."

Mayne slowly nodded. "Yes, I know about the legend. It was my father who excavated the cave. Legend said that the first settlers believed there was a dark spirit living in that cave and they were using it as their form of judgement. If a person were to commit a crime against the tribe, they would imprison that criminal, sealing that cave for a day. If that person was guilty of the crime, then that person would vanish. If not, then he would be spared."

"Then there was the faith healer." Alice added. "He discovered a way to control the dark spirit so that he could decide a tribe member's fate. This caused the Chief of the tribe great unrest as innocent people kept disappearing, or as it was written, 'eaten' by the dark spirit. When the faith healer gotten so addicted to his newfound power, he actually plotted a way to remove the Chief from this plane and become the new ruler."

"But he was founded out," Mayne continued, "they threw the corrupted faith healer into the cave and sealed the entrance, leaving him for dead and hoping the dark spirit had taken him."

"What I'm trying to say, Father, is that what was happening around town may be similar to what the legend says."

"That's preposterous," Mayne said with a slight laugh. "You know that there's no such thing as ghosts except for the Holy Spirit. Besides, when my father removed the seal of the cave, there was nothing there besides this medallion I'm wearing."

Mayne showed Alice the circular medallion with a crucifix on top of it. To the old priest, it may be some sort of faith amplifier, but to Alice, it looked like some cheap trinket that could be bought at the gift shop.

But Mayne made also a point that the legend of the cave was not relevant to what was going on around Greensburg. What Alice saw at Jason Baker's garage did not look like a spirit. It was more like a manifestation of her boyfriend's sin of committing murder and probably pulled him into his own darkness, his own hell.

That made Alice realized that Carol Graham, William Cummings and Jason Baker may still be alive, but not in this world, but to wherever that thing had taken them.

"But I should advise you, Alice," Mayne said before taking another sip of his coffee and slowly gripping his medallion as if he was searching for some form of hope within his own faith. "It would be better not to meddle with this matter any longer. It could be dangerous enough to even cost your life."

Alice knew that too well. But she believed that the police may be way over their heads when it comes to dealing with a supernatural being and only she, Alan and even Jake were more aware of what was happening than anybody else in this town. Yes, it may be dangerous to dig even deeper, but finding a way to put an end to this madness and get back to normal was Alice's goal. If the police could not handle it, who else could?

Alice drank the rest of her coffee and got up from her chair. "Well, I better go see how both Jake and Alan are doing. Thank you for the coffee, Father."

"You're quite welcome, my dear." Mayne smiled in which in a few seconds turned into a sincere and worried expression. "And promise me you and your friends won't go any further with this. I would hate to lose someone like you by the hands of this foul creature."

Alice noticed that Mayne was still gripping on his medallion but even tighter. His heart spoke from within, praying that Alice, Alan and Jake would stay safe until the whole thing is solved. But Alice cannot promise something like that, since the darkly creature had been going after Jake recently. It may had taken her boyfriend, but someone as kind and caring as her classmate Jake Miller, would be someone she could not afford to lose.

"Don't worry, Father." Alice said with a somewhat lying smile, trying to hide the truth. "I have much as much faith in God as I have in you."

Alice walked out of Pastor Brian Mayne's office and out of the church heading toward the hospital. The old priest sat in the chair, still holding on to the medallion so very tightly that it his hand began to hurt.

"For your sake, my child," Mayne whispered to himself, "I sure hope you do.

Alan walked out of the hospital to catch some of the clear, summer air. He then grabbed his cell phone and checked for any messages, since it had to be turned off while inside the hospital. He received one from Alice.

'Just got out of the church,' it read. 'I'll be at the library to check something.'

Alan opened his cell phone and pulled open a hidden keypad underneath. 'Going to have lunch with Sheriff Barkley at the bar,' he typed. 'It's the anniversary of that kid's death today. I'll see you a bit later.'

After sending the message out, Alan turned off his cell and walked back in to see Jake. Arriving at his room, he noticed that Jake was holding some kind of letter and he had uncertain look on his face.

"What you got there?" Alan asked.

Jake tried to hide contents of the letter away from his friend. "It's nothing," he lied. "It's just a 'Get Well' letter."

Alan slightly nodded. "I'm gonna go and have lunch at the tavern. Sheriff Barkley's supposed to be there, anyways."

"There's a small food court down the hallway from here."

Alan grimaced a little. "Yeah, but reminds me of the cafeteria food back in high school."

The two friends laughed a little.

"When are you able to leave?" Alan asked.

"Well, I don't have any physical injuries except being a bit stiff. So I should be able to get out this afternoon."

"That's good to hear. Well, I'll see you later."

Alan was about to step out of the room.

"Oh, Alan," Jake called him back. "Thanks. And tell Alice that…" There was slight pause Jake somehow was able to show a sign of concern for Alan's little sister and a touch of relief after knowing what happened that night at Jason Baker's place. "Tell her that I'm fine, and that I'm glad she's fine too."

Alan had already received the message by Jake's expression. Despite having his sister dating a one-track minded, sports fanatic boyfriend, he could tell that Jake had been showing some fondness toward her over the past few years and he didn't seem to mind it at all. He would rather see Alice dating Jake instead of Jason, but Jake was known to be too shy and possibly nervous when it comes to dating women. He knew that because he was like that too until his dream of become a police officer had given him enough courage, since it's a police officer's job to help everyone, including beautiful teenage girls.

"You got it, buddy," Alan said before stepping out of the room.

Chapter 4

GREENSBURG'S tavern had its days and nights. The exterior looked old and a little run downed with old neon lights attached on the other side of the window on the main door. Of course, it could only be seen lit up at night. Not many people stopped by during the day. But during the nightly weekends, the bar was always packed with hunters, fishermen, and sometimes, even police officers who would go off duty and enjoy a beer or two before heading home to their loved ones.

The interior was no different. Although the same size as the town's diner, the inside of the bar looked ancient with wooden walls, nearly polished tables, an ancient jukebox playing some old country music and only one pool table at the far left side. The bar counter wasn't as large as the one at the diner either. It looked just as old as the tables themselves. Dark brownish colour and a plain shape, the bar counter had been regularly cleaned by the barkeep and owner, Jessica Walker.

A small chime rang above Alan as he walked inside. After a quick look around, he spotted Sheriff Clarence Barkley sitting at the bar counter and Jessica Walker cleaning up a section of it.

After hearing the chime, Jessica spotted the suspended deputy. "Hey, Alan," she waved with her towel.

"What's up, Jessica?" Alan waved back.

Sheriff Barkley looked behind him and spotted Alan walking toward the bar counter.

"What's going on, Alan?" Barkley spoke softly with a half grin.

"I'm doing fine, sir," Alan replied. "Thought I'd come by after lunch since I knew you'd be here on this day in particular."

Barkley nodded at what Alan meant. It had been several years since that day at Carlton City, when he was with the police department, there. That day when he and his former partner, Jeremy Miller, were about to get something for lunch, a nearby convenient store was suddenly robbed. He and Jeremy chased after two masked thieves, armed with pistols and automatic weapons. After being shot at Barkley wanted to injure one of them with a leg shot, but the intensity of rapid bullets hitting around him caused the ageing cop to lose concentration and his target. Although he did pull the trigger, the bullet that escaped from his standard-issued 9mm decided to fly through one of the thieves' head. But Barkley had wished he did not unmasked one of the dead jewellery thief, since it concealed the identity of a young boy who he had saved from a house fire.

"And it's not just that kid either," Barkley spoke before taking a small drink of his beer.

Alan paused a bit before sitting on a stool next to Barkley. Of course, it was also the death anniversary of his daughter. From what Alan had heard she died of a heroin overdose while she was attending university in Carlton City. The poor girl wanted to be a hair stylist and she was only one year away from graduating. Her death happened about three months after the suicide of Olivia Miller Chambers, Jake's mother.

"Well, Sheriff," Alan said softly, giving Clarence Barkley a slight pat on his right shoulder. "You have my condolences."

"Thanks, Alan," Barkley said after taking another small drink from his beer. "I really appreciate that."

"What will be, Alan?" Jessica asked politely.

"Just a sandwich and whatever beer he's drinking."

Barkley chuckled, "Are you sure you're old enough to drink?"

"Do I really need to show you my ID?"

Both men laughed. Alan and Barkley had shared their times in the town's bar from time to time, including on Fridays. They would both sit together and talk about different things. Barkley would keep jabbering about his hunting trips and fishing vacations even though Alan was more of guy who prefers race cars and different performance motors. This didn't bother Barkley one bit since he did like watching a few races on television and those hot supermodels that appear with different racing models.

Barkley noticed the sling and his right arm in a cast that Alan was wearing and began to feel a bit awful for suspending one of his top deputies. He was following the law to the letter, by the letter. Ever since he got transferred from Carlton City, his harsh attitude and barking acts of leadership had made the town safe and quiet over the years being Sheriff of Greensburg. But after seeing what was going on recently around his town and what he saw at Dr. William Cummings's house, he was actually beginning to feel like an actual believer, just like his former deputy sitting next to him, eating his sandwich.

"How are you making out?" Barkley asked.

Alan wiped some crumbs from his lips with his left thumb. "I'm doing alright. Jake's doing fine."

"I heard about it from that deputy that was with you. I've never seen him so spooked like that."

Alan turned his eyes toward the Sheriff. "What about Jason Baker?"

"We're searching around his house, in case he would show up like that Hanna girl. Plus we collected the arm that he may have lost."

Alan nearly chuckled at Barkley's misconception. "Actually, I prefer to say that he did lose an arm. I was there when it happened."

Barkley only nodded. It was true that Alan was there, unless his right wouldn't be broken. "And how's your sister doing?"

Alan washed his throat down with some of his beer. "She's doing alright. A little shaken about Jason's arm falling on her lap like that. She's at the library right now, looking through some stuff. What are you gonna do about Old Man Peterson?"

"Pastor Mayne will make the funeral arrangements."

Alan chuckled, nearly choking on his food. "I'm not sure if there is going to be a funeral, since no one in this town liked him."

Barkley nodded again. His thoughts about his daughter's and the child's death came into his mind and turned himself toward the young man on his right.

"I'm gonna stop by to see my daughter for a bit," the sheriff told Alan, "and later on, I'm gonna head out to the city."

After hearing that, Alan quickly turned his head toward the sheriff. "You're heading out to Carlton City? Then who's gonna look after the town?"

Barkley did not answer. All he did was staring at Alan with that half-a-smile. Alan didn't catch it, but after a small moment, he suddenly knew who will watch over the town while the sheriff is out of town.

"Listen, Allan," Barkley said, "I know that I've gone overboard last night. But whatever the hell is going on around here with these disappearances, dark prints on walls, or even Jason missing an arm, it looks like I can't deny that there's some fucked up shit going on here. And with me out of town, I can't seem to find one officer of the Greensburg Police Department capable of handling a Sheriff's job."

Alan's eyes and mouth widened. He had never felt so glad after hearing those words from his long-time mentor. "Thank you, sir" he said happily with a sense of duty in his heart. "I'll do my best."

"Now, finish your lunch and go grab your badge and gun from my desk. That's an order."

"Yes, sir," Alan saluted to his sheriff.

Barkley left the bar as Alan continued eating. Jessica watched the barely-retired lawman walked out of the establishment with slight shook of her head.

"Poor Sheriff Barkley," she said feeling a bit sorry for him.

"Yeah," Alan said. "It's a real shame for him to lose his daughter like that."

"It's not just that," Jessica glanced at Alan. "From what I've heard, his daughter was once raped by some street thugs. She was only twelve years old at the time."

Alan suddenly felt surprised. "Raped at the age of twelve?"

"And to make matters worse, Barkley suspected it was that same kid that did it, but he had no evidence to prove it. He believes that the justice system in Carlton City was so bad that sometimes the local police wouldn't file a rape case because they were too busy with gang wars and drug trafficking. And the news about his daughter died of heroin overdose only adds fuel to the already burning Sheriff."

Alan was still confused over the story, in which made him more concerned about Barkley. He would have to find out all the details about it, starting with that house fire, that kid he rescued, down to when he shot him down after an armed robbery. He wanted to know more than what Sheriff Barkley had told him, and in order to do that, he would have to follow Barkley to Carlton City to find out.

Alan's cell phone vibrated in his pocket. He picked it up and looked at the small LCD screen. Alice had sent him a message: *Alan, I found something. Meet me at the library as soon as you can.*

Alan finished up his lunch and paid Jessica for the food and beer.

"Keep the change," Alan said to Jessica with a wink.

"I'll see you later," Jessica said back as she watched Alan walk out of the bar, on his way to the Greensburg library.

Chapter 5

JAKE was able to get out of the hospital, that afternoon. As soon as he walked out through the main doors, he felt the warm, fresh air surging in his lungs. The signs of summer were there as the sky was clear and the sun shining brightly onto the town of Greensburg. He had never felt that moment of bliss in his life before. For all the things that occurred in the past few days were hectic enough for anyone to stop and smell nature's fragrance, even for just a second.

Doctor Chandler walked out of the hospital and stood next to Jake, sharing that same moment of bliss.

"Did you have a thought of what you wanted to do now that you've graduated from school?" Jake's family doctor asked as he watched a few birds flew by.

Jake shrugged and slowly shook his head. "I had an idea, but now I'm not so sure anymore."

Chandler smiled a bit, remembering the last time he had asked Jake that question.

"The last time you told me you we're going to be a detective like your father," Chandler said.

Jake remembered that time when he visited the doctor for a routine check-up when he was still six years old, before his father was killed.

"Yeah," Jake said, as he also remembered the reason why he did not want to become a detective. After losing his father, it became clear to Jake that it involves dangerous work. Dangerous, as in getting shot at by criminals. "Now, I'm not so sure anymore."

Chandler understood what Jake meant about that since the doctor knew about Jeremy Miller's death. A tragedy like that could change a child, changing his or her own mind as their own goal in life.

"Well, if you don't want to solve cases," the doctor continued, "why not make them up yourself? I heard that you like to write stories about unexplained mysteries and unsolved cases, right?"

Jake had never mentioned about his own passion of becoming a mystery writer. Probably his aunt Laura may have told Chandler. Every night before going to bed, he would sit at his desk with a small lamp next to him with lead pencils stacked into what it looked like a small wooden potato barrel that he had gotten as a gift from Alan's grandfather.

"It's less dangerous than solving the real ones we have going on in this world," Jake said, turning his glance toward his doctor.

"Jake," Doctor Chandler said, turning toward his sixteen-year-old patient with mildly concerned look, "your aunt and cousin are the only relatives you have, here. I think it would be best to leave everything to the police rather than risking your life for answers in which they are right in front of you."

Jake did not approve of what his doctor was trying to say.

"What am I supposed to do?" Jake said. "I can't just sit at home and wait for my own shadow to come alive again. There's got to be a reason why this is happening to me. And the only thing I can think of is ten years ago, after my mom's suicide. There's got to be a reason why that thing appeared in my mom's bedroom. It may also prevent any further abduction. I believe it has something to do about our worst sins."

Jake began to think about the nightmare, how his own shadow was speaking to him saying that there will be no sin. He still couldn't figure it all out. The only way to find answers would be to go to the old house where he and his mother had lived and meet up with this stranger who had given him the letter.

"Please, Jake," Chandler said, hoping for his determined patient to change his mind. "I would hate to see you in the morgue. Think about your aunt Laura and you're little cousin. We've already lost a good student of Greensburg High School, and I don't think the town is ready to lose another."

Yes, the loss of the school's valedictorian, Karen Hannah was a horrible tragedy for the townsfolk, including her parents. Still, no one could understand how she ended up between her bedroom floor and the living room ceiling. Carol Graham, William Cummings and Jason

Baker had disappeared completely, except with Jason losing an arm in the process.

"Don't worry, doc," Jake said with a huge sigh, trying to reassure the doctor with a simple lie. "I'm not going anywhere."

A smile was formed on Doctor Chandler's face, feeling a bit relief of Jake's words.

"I'm glad to hear that."

Laura and Becky walked out of the hospital and spotted both Jake and Doctor Chandler outside.

"Want to go for pizza later on, Jake?" Laura asked her nephew. "I heard that's the diner's weekend special. Though if you want to stay home, I'm pretty sure they can do take-outs."

Little Becky tugged on her mother's shirt. "Better not have any anchovies, mom."

Jake laughed. "Don't worry, about it Becky. I don't think they serve anchovies to little squirts like you."

"I told you I'm not a little squirt," Becky said, annoyed by her big cousin's teasing.

"A nice twelve-inch will do nicely for all three of us, right?" Laura suggested.

Jake nodded. "I guess so. But before we head home, I want to go see Mom and Dad for a bit."

Laura replied with a nod. She could tell Jake missed them that much, which is why Jake would visit their graves frequently.

"You take it easy, Jake. You hear me?" Doctor Chandler said, tapping Jake's right shoulder.

"Sure, Doctor Chandler," Jake replied. "I promise I won't do anything rash."

Greensburg's local library was pretty small, not like your average place to have thousands of books all organized and in alphabetical order. At least it was small enough to have the history of the town, local legends and popular folklore. The rest were books written by talented authors, half of them dead, most of them still alive. Others were just children's encyclopaedias, research books and the like.

Alice was looking over several history books on Greensburg. Some of them were scattered around on a table in front of her. But the one she had in her hand was a book of Greensburg's legends. More specifically, the one about the town's tourist attraction known as The Black Cave, also known as The Cave of Conviction.

Alan walked into the building. The interior looked very old with wooden shelves with old books, showing wear and tear on their jackets. As for the soft cover ones, the glue it was used for binding looked old, as if only had little strength to hold the pages together.

Alan looked around for a moment, and then he suddenly spotted Alice in the History section. He walked up to her as Alice noticed that her big brother had his deputy uniform on, along with his badge attached onto his left breast, and his standard-issued 9mm handgun tucked in its holster on his right hip.

"You're back on duty?" Alice asked, happy to see her brother in his uniform again.

"Yes, ma'am," Alan replied with a wink. "Sheriff Barkley had finally understood what was going on after all. And speaking of the Sheriff, he decided to have me look over the town while he's gone to Carlton City."

"Sounds like you're up for a promotion."

"I will be taking over as soon as Barkley retires from his duty as Sheriff, by the looks of it. In which case won't be long, now."

Alice was glad to hear the good news about her brother's upcoming promotion. Having the responsibility of maintain the town's peace is a huge job. But with a small town like Greensburg, quiet, calm, and relaxing, it would make the job a lot easier.

"What do you got, Alice?" Alan asked referring to the book Alice was looking at.

"It's the legend of the Black Cave," Alice pointed out. "The first natives used it as their form of judgement. It said that a dark spirit had lived in that cave for centuries."

"Yeah, I heard about the legend. But what does that got to do with the recent abductions?"

"Why do you think it's called the Black Cave at times?"

Alan shrugged but decided to give a simple answer. "Because the interior walls of the cave were so dark that not even flashlight would reveal their true, rocky colours."

"It's not just that. The members of the tribe who committed crimes were sealed in that cave for a day. If that person is found guilty, he would disappear and leave a silhouette of himself on the cave walls."

Alan's eyes widened. "You've got to be kidding me. Karen Hannah and the others had left a black print on the surfaces in which their shadows would be."

"There's more to it," Alice continued, "the tribe's faith healer acted as the tribe's judge. It turned out it was him that was controlling the dark spirit in the cave with some type voodoo magic. They said that he was able to look into other people's souls from within their own shadows in order to find those who would desecrate the tribe's law."

"In other words, someone is actually controlling this thing and targets people who had done terrible things in the past."

"When I was talking to Pastor Mayne, I thought at first it was going after people who break the Ten Commandments. But of course, if this thing were to target those Commandment breakers, the whole town would have been wiped out by now, since everyone here had lied more than once in their lives."

Alan paused for a minute, and then his thoughts suddenly were on Sheriff Barkley. Fear had driven up through his body as he had realized who may be the shadow demon's next target.

"Holy, shit," Alan exclaimed. "I got to go find Sheriff Barkley."

Alan was about to leave as Alice flipped a page in Greensburg's history book. Alice gasped at a sketch in which the shape of the object was so familiar to her.

"Oh my God, Alan," Alice called her brother back. "Take a look at this."

The drawn sketch was a depiction of a circular relic. A medallion of some sort was shown with four circular gems, one on each corner of the relic. Words were written on the outside of the sketch, each pointing to their respective gem. Clockwise, the gems read as Earth, Wind, Fire, and Water.

"It looks exactly like that medallion that Pastor Mayne is wearing," Alice noted.

"You think that the town priest had something to do with the abductions?" Alan asked.

"I don't know, but I will go see him a little later. Though I won't mention about that gift he had gotten from his father until we have solid facts."

"Alright, I'm going to go find Barkley before it's too late."

Alan quickly walked halfway toward the front doors of the library.

"What are you talking about, Alan?"

Alan stopped for a minute and looked back at Alice with a worried glance. "I think Barkley may be the next on this thing's 'snatch list.'"

Jake stood in front of the graves of both Olivia and Jeremy Miller, offering them both a silent prayer before speaking normally to them.

"Hey, guys. It's me again. I just came to tell you something that may be important."

Jake took out the letter he had gotten from the stranger from his jacket pocket.

"Someone came to visit me while I was at the hospital. I'm not sure if I should trust him or not. But he may have answers to the recent abductions that happened in town. He said that mom's got something hidden in the old house, somewhere."

Jake looked slowly toward his mother's gravestone.

"And that night, when you took your own life, there was something there. That shadowy thing was there. I know because Doctor Chandler had told me that Aunt Laura had found me lying unconscious covered in some black liquid. That thing came to me twice, both after Karen Hannah's funeral and while I was in jail."

Jake went closer to his mother's gravestone, begging for some sort of reply. "What is that thing, mom? Did it come after you? And why did it go after me? What is so special about me?"

Laura nearly heard her nephew's plead for answers from inside the car. Of course, she knew what he was talking about. But she had promised her dead sister to keep something from him for as long as she could. But his determination to find the truth to why Olivia had killed herself, and his first encounter with the shadow demon at the age of six, was strong. He would risk anything, even his own life to find the truth. But in this day and age, finding truth may cost something even greater than telling it.

Jake heard a noise, a ruffling sound of bushes nearby. He turned toward the source of the sound only to have spotted a tall man in a dark trench coat and dark glasses. It was the stranger from the hospital, the one who gave the letter to Jake.

The stranger suddenly turned tail and began to run off. Jake went after him, only to have disappeared after making a darting right turn passed a large tree. He vanished like a ghost and with no trace of the stranger whatsoever.

"Jake," Laura called out from her car as she witnessed the brief chase across the cemetery. "What's wrong?"

Jake looked around again, hoping to see the stranger pop up from a concealed hiding place. He shook his head started walking back to the car.

"Nothing, Aunt Laura," Jake said. "I thought I just saw someone spying on me."

Jake climbed into the passenger seat of the car after doing a final quick look around the cemetery. No, the stranger had completely gone.

"Maybe you're just being a bit paranoid after what you've been through," Jake's aunt said as she started her ignition.

"Yeah, I may be. But whoever that was, he looked awfully familiar."

.

Chapter 6

JAKE and his relatives sat around the dining table eating their take-out pizza. His aunt Laura noticed he was chewing his slice very slowly. He had something on his mind, but after what he had been through, she would not dare to ask.

"Aunt Laura," Jake suddenly spoke, still having a small piece of his pizza in his mouth. "Did mom ever leave anything to you?"

"What do you mean?" Laura replied with uncertainty.

"I mean did she leave any valuables, like jewellery or something like that?"

Laura tried to recollect her thoughts after her sister's funeral. "Well, your mother was not big on jewellery. After the funeral, we pretty much grabbed everything that was in the house and sold them to pay for the funeral. Why did you ask?"

Jake shrugged a little while still gazing into his mind. "I was just curious."

Laura sighed quietly. Her nephew still looked determined to find answers. No matter how many times they had told him, he still would not accept that his mother had committed suicide by depression. Jake may have only known his mother during his first six years, but he knew her enough that she would not take her own life. Even Laura knew she would not do something like that and leave her six-year-old child abandoned and being taken care of by his relatives.

Jake took a bite of the crust of his slice of pizza, in which was stuffed with mozzarella cheese, and then turned his gaze at his aunt for a minute. "What about memoirs or diaries?"

Laura knew he was going to ask her that. She thought about it for a minute, and then it struck her about something that she had given Olivia as a gift after moving to Greensburg.

"Well," Laura said, "I do remember giving your mother something when you two moved into this town. It was large notebook, a journal of some sort."

Come to think of it, Jake did remembered walking into his mother's bedroom and seeing her writing down something in a large notebook at times. But she had always hid it somewhere in her bedroom.

"You're not seriously thinking of going to that old house and look for it, are you?" Laura asked, hoping that Jake would give her a good answer.

Jake failed to do so with his silence and his brief glance at his aunt.

"Oh come on, Jake," Laura's hands dropped to the table. "Why can't you just let it all go?"

"I can't deny the fact that there is some connection between what happened ten years ago and what's happening around town. I need to find out the real truth."

"We've already told you the truth, Jake. Your mother committed suicide due to extreme depression. You went into traumatic shock when you saw her body and fell unconscious which made you lose a portion of your memory."

Jake quickly stood up angrily, trying to block out in what he was hearing were total lies. "Yeah, well, you never told me that I was covered in that black shit when you found me there."

"Jake, mind your language!" his aunt snapped. It was true that she had never told him. After hearing what happened to him when he was in jail, she figured that Jake would have known about it since his doctor was the one who got rid of the black bile when she brought him in the hospital ten years ago. "I went to visit you that morning and I found both of you, there. You were covered with this black stuff and you were gasping and wheezing for air, as if your lungs were filled with it. I brought you into the hospital as quick as I could, that's all."

"You could have at least let me die in there with mom," Jake murmured as he left the dining table to go into his room.

A little later, Jake sat on his bed, reading the letter the stranger had given to him. He skimmed through the lines over and over as he was thinking about actually meeting the stranger at the old house and recover the journal that his mother may have hidden.

He then gazed upon the picture frame of him and his parents, sitting on the night table beside him. After picking it up, his thoughts of his parents came into mind as he whispered to the two people that had given birth to him.

"I know this sounds risky," Jake said, "but I need to know everything. I'm pretty sure that your last thoughts and feelings are written in that journal that Aunt Laura had given you. I think that is probably why you didn't write them down on a letter for her or to both of us. But can I really trust this man? He may know the answer to all of this, but I am betting my own life that he may have the solution of preventing anymore abductions from happening."

Jake placed the picture frame back on the night table. He got up from the bed and snatched his school bag. He unzipped the top zipper and opened the bag for his heavy-duty flashlight to be stored in.

There was a knocking on his bedroom door. It carefully swung open to reveal little Becky's pony tails and a concerned look on her adorable face.

"You okay, Jake?" Becky asked. "Are you still mad?"

Jake sighed as he spotted his little cousin in the doorway. "No, I'm not mad, Becky. I'm just disappointed that people are keeping secrets from me."

Becky walked in. Jake zipped back his backpack and placed it on his bed.

"I don't want you to go," Becky said with a bit of sadness in her expression.

Jake knew that if he were to go to the old house alone, there would be chances that his own shadow would show up again in any moment, since it was almost night time.

Jake kneeled down at Becky's level.

"I have to, Becky," Jake confided in her. "It may help figure out what we are dealing with here."

"But you may not come back, after. And I don't want to lose another friend."

Becky was referring to her dying friend Amanda. Jake knew what his cousin meant. It may be devastating for her to lose her best friend, but having to lose another, a relative to be precise, would be even worse.

"I'm already losing Amanda and I don't want to lose you too." Becky's eyes began to water. She cared for her big cousin as much as if he was her big brother. And she had been known to touch the hearts of other people around Greensburg. But seeing her cry in front of him, it had already touched Jake's heart.

Jake let Becky cry in his arms. But even with the plea of an eight-year-old child was not enough for him to change his mind about his ultimate goal.

"Don't worry about it, Becky," Jake said. "I'll be back before you know it. You just have to keep me sneaking out in the middle of the night a secret from your mother, okay?"

"Okay," Becky wiped the tears off her face. "You promise?"

Jake swallowed hard. A promise like that would be difficult to keep, as he was not certain what will he find at the old house or what will happen if he would meet the stranger. But he couldn't say no to an innocent child like Becky Chambers. His aunt and cousin were the only family he had left. He would have to lie about his return, just to keep his cousin smiling.

"I promise."

Chapter 7

JOSH Franco was the child's name. Born and raised in Carlton City by his loving parents Mark and Linda. They had known Clarence Barkley for a long time, since they had been next door neighbours.

Mark was originally from Chile as car dealer until he had the opportunity to transfer to the US, in which he had enjoyed most of his life. He had quickly met and fell in love with a Canadian painter, Linda Brandon and gotten married in Manitoba, Canada.

A year later, they decided to move into Carlton City, New Brunswick, gave birth to their first-born son Josh, and their first daughter, Emily. The family were happy in Carlton City, despite its ever-growing state of crime and corruption and having a member of the Carlton City Police Department living next door to them gave Mark and Linda a sense of security.

Barkley's daughter, Rose and Josh became good friends right away and they would walk to school and back together along with little Emily.

But I was during sometime when Clarence was wondering in the city streets that he had noticed something about Josh. Once in a while he would get a glimpse of a group of young men standing in a corner of an alley, and fourteen-year-old Josh was among them, laughing and screaming like they were a bunch of good friends hanging out. That was when Clarence saw Josh holding something in his hand. A giant, fancy-looking knife, curved at the edge with the handle, sleek and smooth, was made out varnished walnut stock.

It either looked hand-made or even expensive, or possibly smuggled or stolen. Seeing that made Clarence question about Josh's outgoings and most likely, the safety of his own daughter. The thought of her hanging out with someone, who may have had friends from the wrong sort of people, almost frightened him.

Twenty years on the force and witnessing the city's putrid stench of society would make any man feel uneasy, especially concerning the security of his loved ones. Clarence's family had their share of robbers and home invaders in the past, but he was always there for his family. And his twenty years on the force had made him change is opinion about crime all together and his tolerance against group individuals who tend to cause some trouble among the city streets and the innocent civilians living within its walls.

Clarence had kept a close eye on Josh for a while, though it did not impress his daughter. She thought that her old man was paranoid to even think that Josh may be hanging with the wrong crowd and may cause some trouble. But Barkley said that he as only looking after the well-being of his only daughter and that he did not trusted Josh since that day he saw him with his friends and that weapon he was holding.

Josh's parents had said nothing about he does during his spare time, except hanging out with some friends. Their son kept saying that he was having fun with his friends during the weekends. Though he never drank, he never smoked, nor did he do any drugs. But Barkley's definition of fun, without drugs and alcohol in play, could mean robbery, mugging, or vandalising.

A month later, Barkley received a call sometime in the afternoon from his department. They had found Rose half-naked and unconscious on the side or the road, bleeding from between her legs. Hearing about his twelve-year-old daughter raped and left to die in the streets nearly made him strangle the phone receiver to death, nearly breaking it. His mind was filled with anger and revenge was already on his mind. And only one name that first came to mind after hearing the dreadful news: Josh Franco.

When in the hospital, Rose said that she couldn't remember what had happened. All she could have remembered was somebody covered her mouth with a wet handkerchief soaked into some liquid in which made her pass out. And when she woke up, she had felt sharp pain in her pelvis and her crotch immensely

Barkley went to his Lieutenant saying that it was Josh Franco and his group of friends were responsible. But he lacked any substantial evidence which proved otherwise. When the forensics department did a sperm test-in which was found inside Rose, the results were negative, clearly stating that the suspects had no criminal record of any sorts.

Seeing all this made Barkley even more furious and he could not deny his accusation toward Josh Franco. If his friends didn't have a criminal record to begin with, then they were able to get one, by crossing the line and raping his teenage daughter.

No evidence, no leads, and the parents act as if Josh had done nothing wrong, his hatred began to grow overtime and the fact that his own police department were incapable of helping him, he began to have thoughts of performing his own act of justice. But doing so may cause him to lose his job and lower his defences for his own family. What could he possibly do?

Sheriff Clarence Barkley drove up into Carlton City's cemetery and parked along the narrow pathway. He got out carrying a bottle of whiskey he had picked up along the way. He began looking around, searching for the tombstone of the fourteen-year-old Josh. It wasn't too far. After passing a few plots and several old stones, he had finally arrived at Josh's.

The tombstone was large and rectangular, decorated with engraved flowers and ribbons. A small recent photograph of Josh was shown at the very middle of the stone along with his name written in marble. The letters were in uppercase and took up most of the face of the stone itself.

Wreaths and bouquet of flowers were seen around the stone and at the base. They were given by his parents, relatives and most of his friends. Barkley never thought that the teenager was loved by many, despite his claims of being the prime suspect of his daughter's rape. But seeing his name and his face on the stone not only made Barkley felt even more guilty for taking his life because he was still a child, but at the same time, he made a small grin as if the little fucker may have deserved it.

"Hey there, Josh," Sheriff Barkley said to the frozen image of his victim. "You know who I am, right? Well you know that this day in particular is the exact date that I lost my daughter. I'm not saying that you're responsible, since you are already dead. I'm saying that it was because of people like you that my own Rose is gone."

Barkley opened his bottle of whiskey and took a huge swig.

"You wouldn't understand how it feels to lose a loved one by heroin overdose, do you?" Barkley grumbled while wiping the excess whiskey dripping from his lips. "But the fact is that it was your fault to begin with. You and your fucking cronies raped my Rose. She was only a fucking child! She was only twelve-years-old, you miserable little piss ant."

Barkley spat right on the child's grave before taking another drink from his whiskey.

"You know," the Sheriff continued, "I'm very surprised that no one knew who started the fire. They did find traces of gasoline but they never found out who it was."

Barkley took another drink of his whiskey. He was already feeling the effects of the alcohol and his mind was filled with flashes of his daughter, her smiles, her innocence, and that dreadful call about her rape. But one memory was when he heard that Rose had died from heroin overdose when she was attending university in Carlton City. He felt he had lost everything, everything that made him a policeman to begin with. He felt that he failed his duty not only as an officer of the law but his duty as being a loving father. And with that in mind, his small, old-aged eyes gazed heavily onto the dead teenager's photo.

"See," Barkley continued, "I know it was you that raped my little Rose. And it was your friends, and their friends that had given her the heroin. You're all bunch of druggies, maggots, and fucking dog turds. Hell, every one of you fucks is the reason this God forsaken city is under so much shit!"

Barkley, feeling a little drunk, decided to step onto Josh's grave. He didn't care that it would disturb it. He wanted to make sure that Josh's spirit was feeling the heavy weight that Barkley had given him, as if he would be standing on the teenager's bony chest, pressing his lungs like a cushion.

"And to make matters even worse," Barkley yelled, "was that my fucking department said that I had no evidence to support my accusation and your parents were acting like as if you were some God-given angel. I told myself three words: fuck the evidence!"

Barkley had given a nod to that fourteen-year-old visage on the tombstone. "Yeah, that's right," he said, somewhat proudly. "I was the one who burned your fucking house down. And why did I save you instead of letting you burn? Because I wanted you to feel what I felt when I received the call about my little Rose. I wanted you to feel the Devil roasting you for that terrible crime you have done. But that day, when you and one of your pals robbed at convenient store? Yeah, I shot and killed you that time, though I was surprised it was you underneath that ski mask. Sure, I felt a bit guilty for killing you, but between you and me…"

Barkley leaned over toward the photo with a devilish look and a menacing, drunken smile. "I believe that you deserved it."

Barkley took another drink of whiskey. Feeling a little bit more drunk than before and couldn't even think straight, he removed his belt, unzipped his zipper and began urinating all over Josh's grave.

"I hope you're thirsty in Hell, Josh," Barkley chuckled. "This is my gift to you. This is what you get for raping my little Rose Barkley, and for having your buddies kill her with fucking drugs."

Though intoxicated, Barkley almost felt like he was enjoying himself, even though all he ever felt is pain and hatred. He would do that to his former superiors at the Carlton City Police Department for not helping him. He would piss all over the commissioner's grave, his former lieutenants and captains. He would piss on all of them until he dehydrates.

Barkley was suddenly startled by a noise, a snap of a twig from behind. He quickly zipped back his pants and pointed his .38 revolver at the source of the sound.

"Come on out," Barkley shouted, nearly shaken and felt a little wet due to his urine hitting his left pant leg. "Put your fucking hand up and show your face."

Alan emerged from behind a nearby bush with his hands in the air. "It's only me, Sheriff."

Barkley let out a huge sigh and lowered his gun. "God damn it, Alan. What the hell are you doing here?"

"I was concerned about you, sir."

"This is none of your goddamn business. I gave you a job to look over the town while I'm gone."

"Sir, I heard everything. Ever since your daughter got raped, all you ever thought of making that kid suffer because you believed it was him. And I bet you that Josh was innocent of that crime."

Barkley shook his head, not wanting to believe Alan's words.

"You don't understand what it's like to lose a child like my Rose by the hands of these fucking cretins!"

"Your daughter may have been raped by his friends, but she died of drug overdose years after you got transferred to Greensburg. And you're blaming a dead teenager for that?"

"I'm blaming everyone!" Barkley shouted loudly, nearly an echo was heard. "I blame this city's police department, their justice system, and every, fucking, slime that lives and breathes from the gutters!"

Barkley turned toward Josh's tombstone with his revolver pointing at the young face on the photo.

"That includes this little turd here," Barkley shouted, squeezing the grip of his revolver like he was strangling a helpless victim.

Barkley pulled the hammer back on the revolver with his furious, drunken eyes, watered with tears. Looking at the smiling face of Josh's photo was like he enjoying watching the old Sheriff in pain, laughing hysterically and tormenting him.

Barkley's mind was filled with an image disturbing enough to make him want to kill Josh over and over again. He would see his lovely twelve-year-old daughter Rose screaming and crying in pain as the fourteen-year-old Josh thrust himself inside her, laughing and howling like a wild animal.

The scene would then shift over to where Rose had grown into a young woman, but lying on a bed motionless and with needle holes in her arms. Josh would be there carrying a needle filled with the heroin drug that had killed her and stab the already deceased Rose in the chest repeatedly, filling her frail corpse with the narcotic with every stab. Josh laughed and shrieked like a crazed madman who escaped from a mental ward, tormenting Barkley continuously, but all that and the rape scene was all in the old Sheriff's delusional, alcohol-filled mind.

"Give me back my daughter, you son of a bitch!" Barkley shouted.

One after another, Barkley's revolver fired a round. The parts of the tombstone exploded into several pieces and dust with every bullet hit. After his bullet chamber was empty, he kept on pulling the trigger, hoping that more shots would fire. But all he heard was several clicks and the top half of the rectangular tombstone had disintegrated, along with the photo of fourteen-year-old Josh Franco.

Barkley turned toward Alan, catching his breath. Alan had noticed that there was a faint mist smoking out of his mouth with his every exhale. But the nightly weather was warm enough for a midnight stroll at the nearby park.

"Is it getting cold out here, or is it just me?" Barkley asked.

Alan saw something moving behind Barkley. Turned out he was casting a shadow over Josh's grave cause by a nearby street light. It stretched forward toward the half destroyed tombstone.

Alan recognized that strange anomaly when he questioned William Cummings for his involvement with the Greensburg High School's valedictorian Karen Hannah.

"Sheriff, behind you," Alan said as he took out his gun from his holster.

Barkley looked behind him and his shadow had finally manifested the distorted face of Josh Franco. His face darkened by the black liquid, his eyes yellow and brighter than the nearby street light, and a disgusting, gaping bullet hole between his eyes. He was crying like several screaming children.

'I didn't do it, I tell you!' the distorted Josh Franco said. *'I didn't rape your daughter. You've got to believe me!'*

Barkley was shocked in horror when he saw Josh's face in his own shadow, trying to convince the ageing lawman that he had no intention of harming his daughter Rose. But Barkley would not accept Josh's plea, even from the teenager's own grave. He aimed his revolver at Josh's ghost, only to hear the failing clicking sound of the gun's hammer.

"Clarence, get back," Alan shouted as he put away his gun and grabbed his flashlight.

After turning it on, the beaming light had hit Barkley's living shadow, directly at Josh's face. The entity shrieked like several banshees as the light began to burn its essence.

But the shadow creature had other plans, and stretched out one of its arms like an octopus and swung right at Alan like a baseball bat. It hit him on his broken right arm, in which Alan flew a few feet away, crashing against the base of a nearby tree. Alan nearly screamed in pain as he almost felt his arm breaking even more as he spotted his flashlight several feet away from him.

Barkley tried to run, but his own shadow grabbed onto one of his legs. He fell hard right onto the ground and was then getting pulled into the dark pool, swirling and swimming on the surface of Josh Franco's tombstone. Seeing the pool made Barkley think that it may be cesspool of his own sin, his own crime.

But how it could be my sin, Barkley had thought. Josh had raped Barkley's little girl and her death that followed ten years after by his friends. Could it be that Josh was innocent after all? And what about the heroin in which Rose had died from? Was that from his friends, or was it from all the fucking slime that lived and breathed within the gutter of Carlton City?

Barkley's feet had already been submerged. It was deeply cold to the touch that they became numb within moments. His legs then followed after, right up to his knees as the old sheriff of Greensburg tried to grab hold onto every piece of ground he could. But as soon as his entire legs were submerged, he decided to attempt one last action.

Underneath his right sleeve was a hidden gun holster which housed a very small pistol, small enough to be loaded with only one bullet, a gift he had gotten from his former partner, Jeremy Miller. He quickly pressed a hidden switch which released the concealed weapon into his right hand and pointed at his menacing shadow.

"I am not leaving this world like this!" Barkley shouted at the entity. "Rose! Your Daddy is coming for you!"

Alan, trying to stand of his feet, looked at Sheriff Barkley after hearing those words. Barkley had his little one-shot pistol shoved deeply in his mouth and his index finger sat gently on the miniature trigger.

"Clarence, no!"

But it was too late; the single bullet nestled in his pistol had already travelled through the back of his skull. His hat flew off almost instantly as the shot roared through the quiet cemetery.

Barkley's shadow released the grip from his victim and fell back into the darkness. It reformed itself back as the sheriff's very own obstruction of light, mimicking his lifeless body at the base of Josh Franco's tombstone.

Then there was silence, and Clarence Barkley, Sheriff of the Greensburg Police Department was no more. His corpse lay still on top of Josh Franco's grave with a huge, bloody hole in the back of the skull. It was a disgusting sight to see, but not as difficult as seeing the Sheriff actually taking his own life with a pull of a trigger.

Alan felt like throwing up after witnessing the whole scene. He had never seen anyone shooting themselves like that before. But he had been with Barkley for a long while, long enough to even having him as a friend. He may have been strict and followed the book, but outside the badge, the gun and the hat, he was just like every hard working man in Greensburg. It was sad to see him go.

Alan walked back to his car and grabbed the microphone from the radio communicator.

"This Deputy Craig," he spoke into the microphone, a bit shaken by the whole experience. "I need a few units and notify the coroner. Sheriff Clarence Barkley is dead. I repeat: Sheriff Clarence Barkley is dead."

Chapter 8

JAKE was able to sneak out of the house when everyone was sound asleep. He crawled out of his bedroom window and climbed down a nearby tree that had a single, sturdy branch reaching out toward the window. He had used this method before when he was young. Whenever he was grounded he would sneak out that way and meet up with his Alan during the middle of the night.

He made it down and started his walk down the street, heading for the old house in which he and his mother had lived. But along the way, he spotted several police cars heading his way, as well as a coroner vehicle. Alan was inside one of the cop cars.

Jake would not waste any time wondering what is was about, but Alan had already spotted his best friend walking along the sidewalk.

"Hey, Jake," Alan called out as he parked the car along the sidewalk.

"Hey, Alan," Jake said. "What happened?"

Alan had a sad and sore expression on his face. "It's Sheriff Barkley. His own shadow was about to take him but he decided to take his own life."

Jake's eyes widened. "Holy, shit. Why would he do that?"

Alan climbed out of the car groaning a little due to his broken arm. It felt as if it had gotten worse when he fell on it after being struck by the Sheriff's demonic shadow. "It turned out he didn't felt guilty about shooting that boy. He blamed his daughter's childhood rape and her drug overdose on him and his friends."

"But he was dead before his daughter was."

Alan shook his head. "He still blamed it on them. He was so stricken with revenge that he even shot several shots at the kid's gravestone. He nearly blew the whole thing away."

Jake shook his head. "That's terrible. Who's going to be the sheriff of Greensburg now?"

Alan shrugged a bit. "Well, I am up for a promotion and Barkley was on his way to his retirement, so it looks like I may be the candidate for it."

Jake made a brief smile. He had felt somewhat proud to have his best friend as the Sheriff of Greensburg. He had the natural talents of leadership shown toward other deputies and having a Sheriff badge would have made Jake a bit more secure, if Jason Baker would still be around to terrorize him as usual.

"Besides," Alan said, "why are you out here this late? You should be home. You never know when that thing might come after you again."

Jake hesitated for a minute, and then he tried to avoid the question by walking away. "Sorry, I've got to go. I have to go meet up with someone." That last bit had slipped out. Jake was a bit surprised that it did, and hoping that Alan didn't catch that.

He did.

"Let me go with you," Alan said.

Jake shook his head. "You can't, Alan. I have to go alone."

Alan paused for a moment and thought about something. "It's about that letter you got, isn't it? It's not just a 'get well' letter."

"Please, Alan. The last thing I wanted was a good friend to get hurt by all this."

"Well it's too late for that." Alan showed his right arm, still in a cast. "Come on, Jake. I can't let you go alone. You need some protection."

"I have a flashlight with me," Jake's voice raised. "That's all the protection I need."

Jake walked another a few steps away from Alan.

"It's my duty as a policeman to protect you, Jake." Alan's voice also rose, sounded annoyed by his friend's rejection from his offer.

Jake turned back toward his friend, growing tired of Alan's offer "Well if it weren't for me," Jake shouted, "you wouldn't be a policeman to begin with." That had slipped out too. He wished he could just shut up and kept walking to go to the old house.

Alan stopped in his tracks, confused for a bit. He shook his head trying to make sense of what Jake said. "What are you talking about?" he asked.

Jake stopped. He closed his eyes and bit his lip. He did not want to answer that, since it may trigger another line of questioning in which may lead to something he had hidden away from his best friend for a long time. He promised himself not to tell Alan about it, his involvement in having Alan being a policeman. It would cost them their friendship if he had told him, but the way the situation had become, he had no other choice. Besides, Alan had to find out sooner or later.

Jake turned back toward Alan and approached him. His lower lip still tucked behind his upper teeth, trying to not let the truth slip through his tongue again.

"You didn't become a cop on your accord, Alan," Jake said, still trying to hold it all back. "I made you into a cop."

*****

Jake couldn't breathe. He couldn't move his head. Large quantities of water from the toilet had already gone through his nostrils and some in his lungs. He tried to escape but his head was held down, submerged by a large hand. The hand was very strong, something that a person who would participate in school's sports would have.

The hand that held Jake's head pulled him out of the water from the toilet bowl. He had noticed the bad breath coming from the hand's owner's mouth, putrid, disgusting and menacing.

"The next time I see you with my Alice," Jason Baker whispered in Jake's wet ears, "I'll make sure to leave you a little present in there. Besides, I've been eating a lot beans recently."

There were sounds of laughter not far from them. Two of Jason's friends were standing near the door of the men's washroom, checking outside to see if anyone important would pass by. The two laughed like hyper-active hyenas and enjoyed every moment of Jason's abuse toward Jake.

Jason released his grip from Jake and re-joined his entourage at the door, leaving Jake to recover any remnants of his dignity. After the bullies left, Jake sat on the cold, damp floor with his knees tucked in against his chest, his arms folded on top and his face planted in his folded arms.

Jake had cried for a long time. He was not sure how much more abuse he could take. Every time Jake ends up talking to Alice, Jason wouldn't be far off, prying his eyes on his prey like an animal protecting its most valuable possession. Even if it was just a simple 'hello,' Jason would not accept that. Alice had tried to reason with Jason that Jake had no intention of stealing her away, but his thick-headed, sports-filled skull had no opening for something like that.

All Jason had believed was winning and going for the prize and to him; Alice Craig was one prize he would keep forever, despite her brother being Jake's personal bodyguard.

A little later, Jake was walking down the street, heading for home. Alan drove up beside him on his bicycle from behind carrying his book bag in a small basket behind his seat.

"Hey, Jake," Alan said. "What's up?"

Jake didn't bother looking at his long-time best friend. His face still had drops of toilet water from his ordeal with Jason Baker, in which Alan noticed why Jake looked gloomy and wet.

"Did something? Happen to you?" Alan asked.

"Just the usual," Jake murmured.

"That fucking jock," Alan sighed. "I don't know what Alice sees in him."

"All I did was saying hi, nothing else. It's like he's watching my every move to make sure I don't get close to her. I can't even make eye contact with her from a distance without him watching me behind the shadows."

Both Alan stopped his bike as Jake stopped walking.

"And you know that any friends of Alice is a friend of mine," Alice assured Jake. "You know that, don't you?"

"But Jason doesn't see that."

Alan placed his hand on his shoulder. "Don't worry about it, buddy. I'm taking that law enforcement test tomorrow. If I pass it, I'll be able to train at the police academy and become a full fledge cop. Then you don't have to worry about that Baker guy."

Hearing that almost gave Jake a sense of hope. Ever since father's death, he had a difficult time coping with the hardships with school. It felt like the protective shield he had carried by his father came crumbling down and all the bad guys waiting on the other side came rushing in like wild, rabid dogs.

Eight years had passed since his father's funeral, and he had the feeling of insecurity since then. But the idea of Alan being a cop would make Jake feel a little more secure, but only if he had passed the law enforcement test. He hoped that Alan would pass, he had to pass. But if he were to fail the test, then Jake would have to endure more abuse by the giant bully until graduation, if he could live that long.

The next day arrived. The law enforcement test took place at the station of the Greensburg Police Department. The test supposed to last around two hours and the passing grade was ninety percent. Just the passing grade itself was imitating enough for Alan to be a little worried. But he would never give up. His dream of becoming a cop and help other people stayed with him throughout his life since he was a child and passing this law enforcement test felt like a rare opportunity for him take that first toward his goal.

Alan, Jake and Alan's father Derek arrived at the police station in Derek's pick-up truck. Alice didn't tag along because she needed to study for exams.

"Well," Alan said to the others, "wish me luck."

"Hope you do pass, Alan." His father said.

"So do I, but if I ever do fail the test, I would have to wait another six months before I can take it again."

Six months? After hearing that Jake, felt a surge of uncertainty and felt a bit worried. Does that mean that Jake would have to suffer through another six months of abuse from Jason Baker? He would rather go through one year of it instead, if Alan would succeed. He wouldn't be able to survive that long.

"I hope you do pass, Alan." Jake said. "We'll keep our fingers crossed."

"Thanks," Alan said, getting out of the pick-up.

Alan was already at the front door of the station. The anxiety was rushing all over his body, making tremble in his shoes. But he had to face the challenge or else he won't get into the police academy. He took a deep breath and exhaled fast, pushing all the anxiety out of him in a large, quick burst. At that moment, he opened the front door and disappeared into the building.

A couple of hours have passed and both Jake and Derek were waiting outside, leaning on the hood of the pick-up truck. Derek almost felt like dozing off but Jake was wide awake due to the suspense and the upcoming result of Alan's law enforcement test. He breathed deeply and whispered a few words repeatedly. Come on, Alan. You've got to pass the test. You've just got to.

The front doors swung open. Alan walked out of the station biting his lower lip. The expression on his face seemed questionable, as if he was uncertain about how the whole test session went.

Jake had noticed Alan's expression and he did not like it. Did Alan pass the test or not?

"How did it go?" Jake asked.

"We'll know the results by tomorrow," Alan said with a disappointed expression.

"Do you think you've passed?" his father asked.

Alan replied with a shrug and a slight shook of his head.

"Oh well," Derek placed his left hand on his right shoulder. "If you don't, there's always next time."

Alan made a slight smirk. "Yeah, I guess so."

Jake just stood there, worried about the results of the test. If Alan failed, than Jason Baker would be on his back through the rest of his remaining school years. He would not survive any more torment if that were to happen. Unless…

"Hey Jake," Derek snapped him out of it. "We're gonna head down to the diner for some burgers. I'm buying. How about you join us?"

Jake slightly shook his head. "No thanks. I was supposed to pick up something at the convenient store for Aunt Laura."

That was an easy lie.

"Okay, another time, then. Catch you later, Jake." Derek waved as he and his son climbed into the pick-up truck and drove off.

Jake waved back as the old pick-up truck lifted the dust and dirt from its rear tires. He had to tell them that particular lie, only to give him an opportunity to execute a certain plan he was able to concoct in a short time. He needed Alan to pass the test, and the expression Alan had given didn't look like he had it easy. There was only one way to find out and that was to walk right into the police station, and find the test papers.

Jake had sworn himself to secrecy and would not mention his plan to Alan as it may cause them both their friendship, but he utterly was desperate. If his own father couldn't protect Jake anymore because he was dead, who else would? All that required was a blue pen, and certain modifications on the tests.

The following day arrived. Derek walked out of the house and went to the mailbox to check for any contents. Only a few bills were found but one envelope had Alan's name printed on the front. On the left corner of the envelope was the address of the Greensburg Police Department. The verdict had come and Derek called out to his son as he walked back inside.

Alan's eyes popped wide open with joy as he read the letter that was concealed in the envelope. He had passed the law enforcement test with flying colours, a perfect one-hundred percent score. He jumped and cheered as his path of becoming a police officer had finally been set. All he had to do was to train and study hard at the police academy for one year.

That year had gone and a ceremony was being held at the football field located behind Greensburg High School. Twenty young men and women stood proudly in their new uniforms, waiting for their names to be called out to accept their badge and their new responsibility to maintain the peace of their hometown.

Alan was among the twenty new officers. His name had finally called out by Sheriff Clarence Barkley. After accepting the badge the sheriff had whispered into Alan's ears saying that he will make sure that he will be stationed at Greensburg and not to be transferred to that dreadful place known as Carlton City.

Jake was among the audience along with his aunt Laura, his little cousin Becky, and Alan's younger sister Alice. Everyone in the audience applauded proudly and cheered. Jake did applaud to Alan's success but he did not cheer. He already knew that his best friend would make it, he made it happen. Though he did felt a bit of regret for what he had done that day after Alan did the law enforcement test, but seeing him up on that platform accepting his badge and his new job as Deputy of the Greensburg Police Department made Jake felt more secure, more safe than ever. And if his father would still be alive, then he would not be afraid of anything, not even getting pounded on by Jason Baker…except maybe telling Alan the truth.

*****

Alan just stood there, shocked and confused. "You did what?"

Jake did not want to say it, but the clues that had slipped passed his tongue had given him no choice but to confess to his best friend about what he did that day. "I've modified the tests, Alan. I did it so you would pass it and be a cop."

Alan was still shocked and confused. He shook his head trying to make sense of it all, but he couldn't believe what he was hearing. His breathing was heavy and a possible surge of anger was growing inside him as he walked up closer to Jake, hoping that what he had heard was only a joke. "You're kidding, right?"

Jake shook his head, trying not to look into Alan's eyes. He had no choice of telling him that. The clues had already slipped through his tongue, and besides, Alan was going to find out sooner or later.

"But I've aced that law enforcement test, I made a perfect score."

"You didn't seem so sure when you walked out of the station. After you and your dad left, I went inside and check for myself. You weren't even going to pass with those answers, not even close enough to earn a fifty."

"The question is why, Jake?" Alan's voice rose with a bit of anger. "Why, you of all people would do that to me?"

There was a brief of silence and Alan was dying to get an answer from Jake. But Jake knew that if he had told him the reason, it would sever their friendship like a sword cutting through a rope. But he had to tell him, either way, he would know.

"I did it because…I needed someone to put between me and Jason Baker."

There was an eerie silence. Alan froze even more but the growing anger and disappointment had freed him from the bonds. Jake Miller,

Alan's long-time and best friend had went up behind his back and modified the tests to make sure he would pass and to become an officer of the law, just so he could have protection against a simple, high school bully.

Alan slightly shook his head as it all became clear to him. "You mean all this time, all this time I'm wearing this badge, I've been nothing but a fucking lie?" Jake had said nothing. "What you've done is considered cheating, you know that?"

Jake felt so much anger in Alan's tone that it was unbearable to keep eye contact. But he nodded slightly at what Alan had said. "I know that what I've done was wrong."

"You God damn right, it was wrong!" Alan shouted. "I could go to prison for this, and it will be your own fault!" Alan turned away and took a few steps before facing Jake again, furious and very upset. "Who would have thought that someone like you would do this to me, and for his own fucking, selfish reason?"

Jake was able to make eye contact since Alan was now several feet away. "I was desperate, Alan. You've got to understand."

"Understand what? That you can't stand up for yourself and fight back against a fucking bully?"

"I've lost my father, Alan. I had no one to turn to until I met you." There was a slight pause and Jake's left right eye began to water. "You're like a big brother to me, Alan. You've been the best friend any six-year-old boy could have asked for. You've always been there, helping people who are in need, being this knight in shining armour around girls including Alice. And seeing you as a policeman had proven that you could make a difference in this town."

"What, this thing?" Alan grasped his badge that was attached to his brown uniform. "It's a piece of shit because of you!"

"I made you into the police academy because I needed someone. I needed someone with me."

Alan shook his head and let out a huff of steam. "I can't be your father, Jake. And what you did back then won't change a thing. From what you told me, how could he still protect you if he stayed at Carlton City after you and your mother moved here?"

Jake had never felt that insulted before, not even by Alan.

"You could say that it was his own fault that he got shot down by gangsters," Alan continued his insults. "If he would have cared about you two a little more, he would have told his superiors to shove his job right up their wrinkly ass. And you mother would still be alive."

Jake's hands turned into fists as he absorbed more insults. He just wanted Alan to shut up about his father.

"Jeremy Miller of the Carlton City Police Department was a selfish man," Alan yelled, "just like you! If he had known better, he would still be with you, teaching you how to stand up to guys like Jason Baker. But no, Detective Jeremy Miller is dead!"

Jake did not want to hear anymore, as any additional insults may cause him to burst out and smack Alan across his jaw.

"His own job killed him!"

That was it, Jake charged Alan at full speed with his left fist up and ready. But Alan was too smart for that approach, as Jake didn't know that at the police academy, they teach on how to defend criminals who are willing to attack an officer. They taught Alan how to dodge, grab onto the flying punch and flip the assailant down to the ground. Alan was pretty quick with that move as Jake flew forward and landed on his back really hard. Alan subdued Jake by pressing his muscular, right leg against his neck, nearly choking him.

"Assaulting an officer of the law is a federal offence, you know that?" Alan growled as he held his former friend to the ground.

Jake tried to break free by pushing Alan's heavy leg away from his neck, but he was too strong for him. The academy had shaped him very well. He was strong enough to even take down Jason Baker with one football tackle, if Jason would still be around and not trapped in the darkness in which his own shadow had taken him to.

Jake looked up with much anger in his eyes. "Who said you were one to begin with?"

Alan slightly nodded. Jake was right. Since it was him that modified the test results in order for Alan to pass, he being a policeman was a total fad, all thanks to Jake's selfish act. "You're right about that. If it weren't for you, I would've arrested you right here and now."

Alan released his grip from Jake and let him stand on his own feet. Jake tried to catch his breath as he tried to sooth his neck. The two former friends looked each other for a minute before Alan gave Jake a fair warning. "I'm going to go find Alice. And if you ever come near either of us again, I will arrest you for harassment. Cop or no cop, I will bust your ass. And don't think I will save you the next time your own shadow tries to take you away."

Jake didn't show any signs of agreement but he knew that what Alan had said was crystal clear as he watch his former friend climbing back into the car and drove off. Their friendship had been lost and had become somewhat close to being enemies. Jake knew he had it coming, and he knew he had deserved it but what he did not deserve were the insults about his father and that had made him just as mad as Alan when he finally knew the real truth of his job.

Jake had already wasted enough time. He was heading for the old house to where he and his mother had lived and to meet up with the mysterious stranger. After gathering the last of his breath, he took his backpack that had fallen off his shoulder during the fight and continued his walk, leaving his friends, his worries and his guilt aside for later as the answers about his mother's death, the abductions and his own life, would come first.

Chapter 9

ALAN arrived at the station still feeling upset by the whole thing with Jake. He had wished it would just go away and pretend that what he had told him had never happened. But the fact that Alan thought that he was living his dream, only to be revealed that it was a total lie, a scam, he felt like giving up.

His father Derek was at the reception desk. He heard about Sheriff Barkley's suicide so he came to make sure it was all true. Derek spotted his son walking in through the front doors.

"Alan, I heard about the Sheriff. Are you alright?"

"Yeah, I'm fine." Alan said to his father, trying to hide his upset expression.

"It's too bad about him. The sheriff was a good man. And I also heard that you were going to take his place when he retires."

Alan shook his head. "I don't think I could be a Sheriff of Greensburg, Dad."

Derek had a sudden puzzled look with a slight grin. "What do you mean? Of course you can, Alan. From what I heard you've shown some form of leadership along with the other deputies. And besides, it gives you…"

"Have you talked to Alice, lately?" Alan interrupted, blocking whatever words of confidence his father was trying to give him, as it kept reminding him of what he had pretended to be.

"No," Derek replied, "Last time I heard she was going to see Pastor Mayne after checking out the library, but that was hours ago."

Alan walked up to his father. Derek's son's expression was clear that he had been into a fight, and not because of Barkley's suicide. "Are you okay Alan?" he asked.

"They will have to find someone else to be Sheriff, Dad." Alan somewhat whispered as he detach his badge from his right breast. "I can't be a cop anymore.

There was some sadness in Alan. Derek tried to comprehend what his son was trying to say. But seeing him handing his badge over to his own father had nearly shocked the middle-aged tow trucker.

"Alan, what are you…" Derek tried to say but his right hand was brought up by his son and the badge sat neatly on his palm.

"I can never be Sheriff of Greensburg if I weren't a policeman to begin with."

Derek froze as he watched his own son walking away from his own dream, his opportunity of being Sheriff, his ability to help people in need and his own pride. He only stopped at the front doors, only to look back at his father one more time before he left the station again.

"I'm going to look for Alice. All call you when I find her."

Jake stood at the foot of a cemented walkway that was linked to both to the street and the small garage. He gazed upon the small, dark, lifeless building of his old home. It was pretty small, small enough to house a small family. The front door lost most of its colour due to age and the windows were boarded up.

Jake remembered whenever he would go to school, both his mother and father were standing in the small porch, waving goodbye as he walked alongside Alan and Alice. Those were the only time that his father had visited him and his mother. The rest was just her, and the after, it was his Aunt Laura at a different home. The smiles on their faces were memorable enough to nearly bring a tear on in his eye, but that was not what he came for.

Jake checked his surroundings with his flashlight scanning around. There was no sign of the stranger anywhere. He checked his watch. It was only eleven fifty at night. Turned out he didn't waste much time after the fight he had with Alan. But the stranger had written in the letter that there was something hidden in the house, most likely some diary or journal according to Aunt Laura.

Jake went up to the front door and turned the knob. Of course, the door would be locked. But he did remember where key was hidden. The three large black numbers, '369' were shown, nailed next to door was the first thing he had thought the key would be. His father modified one of the numbers to have a secret compartment within the wooden. A rusty nail on the '6' was visible and plain to see. But Jake knew that the nail was only a disguise. He pressed onto the nail and pushed it downward.

A small, cubical space was carved inside the number and the real nail was inside to keep the number up. A small, brass key was hanging by that same nail, waiting for Jake to be picked up and use it on the old keyhole above the door knob. The key slid into keyhole perfectly and with a twist, the latching sound of the lock was heard, and the door knob turned easily.

The front door made a creaking sound as it was being pushed opened. Jake beamed his flashlight inside. It was really dark, even darker than the night outside. There was no furniture insight, no chairs, no sofas and no TV's left behind. They had really taken everything out of the house after his mother's funeral.

The air was muggy and dusty, like it hasn't been clean for years. But Jake's memories of his time here were still fresh, just as if it was yesterday. His aunt Laura would watch TV with him in the living room, his mother cooking up some sweets in the kitchen, and his father would be out in the garage doing some repairs on Mom's car. But that was before the phone call.

Yes, Jake remembered it too well, when his mother was waiting for him to arrive during their wedding anniversary, she had thought he stood her up. But the reason was that her husband had been killed by a drive-by gang in Carlton City while on his way to see his family. That was when everything changed.

Jake looked around some more, glancing at the remnants of his mother's dusty and dead kitchen, the old bathroom near the stairway and back at what used to be the living room. In front of him were the stairs that lead to his old bedroom, a second bathroom and his mother's bedroom, the room where Olivia Chambers Miller had taken her own life.

Jake carefully walked up the staircase. As soon as he was at the top, the memory of that night had triggered. Though he could not remember what happened before that, but he could recollect the time when he got up from his bed with a sore right cheek. He was heading for the toilet when he was hearing some creaking noises, like the sound of an old rocking chair, but the creaking sound sounded metallic, not a wooden at all. Jake followed the same footsteps he had taken ten years ago. Curious of where the sound was coming from, he slowed his steps, making sure that he would not make a sound.

The hallway stretched across and it would turn at a ninety-degree angle to the left. The window on the wall above was boarded up but Jake remembered that there some light coming in from the nearby street lamps. And he did remembered that it used to rain heavily before, but there was no rain at all. Only the deathly silence and that creaking sound kept playing in his mind like a broken record.

Jake followed the path and turned to the left. There was a door there, but it was opened all the way toward the inside. He remembered what he saw when he pushed it open. The creaking noise, a lifeless body hanging on the ceiling lamp by an old yellow rope that used to belong to his mother, and then there was the black out.

Jake walked into the room with his flashlight beaming across every surface. The old bedroom was dusty and damp. The desk next to the bed frame was still there. That was where his mother sat and wrote her journal. If she would be writing it there, then she would have hid it in the desk somewhere.

But before Jake could search the desk for the journal, he took another look up at the ceiling lamp. It was bent in one side, due to the weight of his mother's body. The old light bulb was still in its socket, filled with puss of dust and dead bugs. Looking at the ceiling lamp made Jake wonder what made his mother commit such act like that and leave little six-year-old Jake to the rest of the world. Could it really be depression, or could it be something else?

Jake suddenly felt something in his mind, something that was hidden from him. Whatever it was, it did not feel good. Another lost memory had begun to manifest in his mind and uncoil itself from the tangled web of his synapses. What is that?

Then he heard a child screaming, similar to the one he heard in his nightmare at the hospital. *'I hate you, I wish you were dead!'* The screaming words kept banging inside his skull. He recognized the voice. It was his own, his own voice from when he was six. At first he thought it was just his mind playing tricks on him because of the nightmare, but it was definitely his own six-year-old voice. But who was he talking to? Was he talking to his own mother?

Finally, his mind had finally cleared up and the manifestation of his lost memory was complete. He had finally remembered what happened between his mother's suicide and the last time she had smiled. But it was that one memory that Jake had wished he hadn't got back. Playing it through his head like a used cassette tape, the events that led to his mother's suicide was revealed to him. He went down on his knees, staring blankly into his own mind with tearful eyes.

"It's my fault," Jake murmured. "It's my fault."

Chapter 10

THE heavens kept on crying, but from the gloomy dark sky above. The rain would not let up for anyone. Not even the poor souls that walked among the Greensburg's streets. Wet, cold, and maybe stricken with pneumonia, the townspeople decided to take shelter from the continuous rain storm and treat themselves with hot chocolate, chicken soup for the sniffling children, and just some much needed rest.

Unfortunately, there were some who cannot rest. Greensburg's local tavern was known to be a bit rowdy during the weekends, especially during hunting season. A few hunters would stop by at night and have several drinks, most likely to celebrate their latest trophy. Among the few hunters was Peterson, Chad Peterson.

Fifty-five year-old hunter was known to be the loudest in every party. He would talk his latest hunting exploits and make crude jokes, but that was when the alcohol had begun to affect his brain as well as some of his manners.

"Hey," Peterson said to his fellow cronies, "You're not going to believe this, but when I was walking by that cave, there were a few tourists. And one of them had biggest, heart-shaped ass I've ever seen. It was just as big as moose's ass. And you wouldn't believe how big her fucking titties were."

"I bet she was some supermodel to have boobs and ass like that," one of Peterson's peers chuckled.

"Are you kidding me? I don't even care if she's a supermodel or some damn milf. I would ride on her big ass and yank on her blond hair like a horse in heat."

Peterson got up from his chair and started thrusting his pelvis in the air. At the same time, he began whipping across his pelvis like he was spanking something. His friends laughed and howled like over-excited drunks, in which made some of the quiet patrons around them felt they were at some zoo.

Jessica Walker was at the bar counter washing some glasses when she overheard the lewd conversation. She felt disgusted by the commotion, which was probably why she never got married. Hearing Peterson and his friends discriminating women like as if they were sex toys was made her one of the toughest. For someone in her mid-forties, she could take any insult any man can throw at her. But she had a wicked tongue and she knew that Peterson and his drunken colleagues had too much to drink for the night.

"Hey, settle down over there," Jessica shouted at the overzealous hunters.

After hearing that, Peterson decided to play with Jessica with some crude words mixed with some slithering due to his beer intoxication. "Hey, Jess," he said to the black-haired barkeep, "How about we go in the back and see if we can mix up some of concoction with our hormones, eh? Since you're not married an all, you would like a man who knows how to handle his gun."

Jessica gave Peterson the finger. "Sorry for breaking your little one-shot pistol, Chad. But I got other work to do than playing with horny cowboys and naked Indian girls."

Peterson's friends laughed at Jessica's one-shot pistol comment in which had nearly insulted the drunken bastard. "Hey, shut the fuck, guys," he yelled. "Anyways, bring me another beer, will ya?"

Jessica placed her drying towel on her left shoulder. "I think you had too much to drink, Peterson."

"If I pass out in here, then you will know I had too much to drink. But I'm still conscious, so bring me another fucking beer!"

I guess, Jessica thought with a sigh. Guess I'll get Olivia to take of that.

"Olivia," Jessica called out. "Would you mind taking care of those assholes?"

"Coming," Olivia Chambers replied as she walked out from the back of the bar.

Olivia felt a little better and a bit more relaxed after being fired from the town's diner. Every night that she punched in, there was a sense of tranquility around the establishment in which helped her easing her mind off the troubles she was having. Sure, she may have lost one job, and maybe finding some way for her to start over her life and move on. Besides, she had a six-year-old son to care for, and she couldn't be even luckier to have a caring, loving boy under her wing. But losing her job at the diner may put a hamper on her financial means as she still had several outstanding debts that her husband Jeremy had left her family after his funeral.

"Hurry up, will ya?" Peterson barked at the red-headed waitress.

Olivia kept asking herself why on this particular night that Peterson and his group of hunting degenerates would be visiting this tavern. The minute the cold, crisp liquid from a bottle makes its way into his system, he transforms from a quiet man to a crazy disrespectful animal. His friends were the same thing.

Olivia quickly grabbed a beer bottle from the nearby refrigerator and walked up to the table to where Peterson and his companions sat. She didn't want to delay any further as it may anger the drunken huntsman and cause a scene.

As soon Olivia placed the bottle on the table, she suddenly felt a huge hand slapping her right buttock. She flinched and turned toward the owner of that hand with instant anger.

One of Peterson's friends smiled and acted like they hadn't done anything. He then looked back at her angered face with a wink. "What's up, honey buns? Been working out lately?"

Olivia didn't say anything. All she wanted was to take that beer bottle and smash it over his head, but that may do more than good, as the hunters looked a bit muscular for all the dead deer and moose they were hauling. All she could do was walk back to the back of the bar.

Jessica saw the whole thing. "Hey," she yelled "Do that one more time and I'll have you thrown out of here."

One of the hunters waved back as if he didn't care. But Peterson had something to say. "Well it's our my fault that you hired a pretty girl like that, Jess," the middle-aged hunter smirked, "We're just trying to get to know each other, that's all."

Yup, Jessica thought, they're all drunk and one more drink will either make them pass out or make things worse.

Jessica walked into the backroom and spotted Olivia stacking trays of glasses. She could tell that her friend was tired and looked paler than before. Well, no doubt, working two jobs tend to wear a person pretty quickly. But sometimes losing one job out of the two may not be a bad thing.

"Are you okay, loved?" Jessica asked her employee.

"I'm fine," Olivia replied quickly.

Jessica gently placed her hand on shoulder, offering some form of comfort. "Don't worry," she said, "Just couple hours left until closing time. And if those sorry asses bother you again, I'll make sure they don't come in this place again. I promise you that."

Olivia looked at Jessica and noticed by her expression that she would stand by her word. Her comforting smile and her tough attitude had made her feel more secure. She could tell that Jessica had her share of drunks and she had thrown a few out of her bar before. That was how she managed to have kept this place open by following simple rules. You can come here and enjoy a few drinks, or drink to your heart's content. But if you started to create scene and harass the employees and/or other customers, you will be advised to leave, or you'll be forced out. If you decided to come back and harass the people even more, the manager will have to contact the police to settle the matter.

But Jessica preferred throwing bad people out the door, since bad customers is bad for business, and sometimes Olivia would share that same strength and courage in order to overcome her own obstacles. But after several months since her husband's funeral, her current strength and courage had almost withered away. And to lose her job at the diner may have been something that she needed, a pause, a moment of rest, a first step of starting over.

Olivia walked back out from the backroom and toward an empty table with empty beer bottles and glasses still sitting on it. But little did she knew, that Peterson was whispering something among his fellow patrons. As soon as he was done he signalled them with a nod of his head and got up from his seat.

Olivia was about to walk back the bottles and glasses in her hands but was suddenly blocked by Peterson's ugly presence in front of him.

"You're name's Olivia, right?" Peterson asked with a sly grin. "Mind if I dance with you?"

One of Peterson's friends popped a quarter in the nearby jukebox. It played something that was a mixture of the blues and country music and Peterson had begun to slightly swing left and right along with the song.

"Um, sorry," Olivia said, tried to walk passed Peterson. "I've got work to do."

Peterson's huge paws had already held onto her arms like a bear in dire need of food. "What's the hurry?" he said. "You don't want to dance with sexy hunter like myself?"

Jessica could not stand it. She suddenly dropped her drying towel on the bar counter and was about to go after Peterson to finally throw him out. But Peterson's goons had other plans.

The minute Jessica got out from behind the bar counter, two large hunters suddenly stood in front of her.

"Come on, Jess," one of the hunters spoke, at least trying to be polite. "Let the man have a little fun."

Jessica tried to walk passed them but one of them was quick enough to latch one of his filthy hands on one of her arms, hurting her in the process. The other got a hold of her other arm.

"Let go of me, you fucking brutes!" Jessica yelled.

"Not until we're done here," one the hunters said. "And you're gonna watch this."

Peterson was able to have Olivia trapped in his arms like a giant beast. He began swinging back and forth with the song blaring out from the jukebox. Olivia tried to break free, but all she could do was yelling and crying.

"Let me go!" Olivia cried out as she watched some of the other customers just sitting there, staring at the whole scene like a bunch of statues. Neither of them had the heart to help her escape. Though they did look worried and concerned and could not figure out what Peterson would do next, neither of the innocent patrons wanted to get involved. They would rather mind their own business and enjoy their beer like as if nothing had happened.

Jessica struggled to get free and help Olivia, but the two hunters were too strong for her, too heavy for her. They were probably too heavy to the throw them out of the bar to begin with. She tried to reach for anything that might help her escape, like an empty bottle or something solid, but they were out of her reach and all she could do is trying to get free while watching Peterson having his way with poor Olivia Chambers.

"Let's have a little more fun, shall we?" Peterson said, before grabbing Olivia's head made her bend over on a table.

Jessica knew what Peterson was going to do to Olivia at that moment. "Let her go, you fucking pig!" she yelled as she watched the drunken hunter pulling down her jeans.

One of Peterson's cronies whistled at the sight of Olivia's pink-skinned backside. "Damn, her ass looked just like they belonged to a school girl, boss."

"Oh, really," Peterson replied to one his friend's comments. "Well then, let's see if she feels like one."

Peterson's friends cheered and howled and Peterson was about to make his way inside Olivia.

Olivia's tears were all over her face and her cries were long and loud. She could not believe what was going on and what was going to happen to her. All she could ever think about was hoping that someone would stop this and set her free. But there was no one. The other customers stood there in shock, Jessica was held back by Peterson's subordinates and Chad Peterson was just moments away from shoving himself inside her. Her arms were spread out across the table and her head was held tight against the wooden table by Peterson's menacing grip.

Olivia suddenly felt something at her fingertips of her left hand. It felt like glass of some sort, rounded and wet. It was an empty beer bottle that was knocked over by Peterson before me made her bend over. Her fingers wiggled furiously, trying to get a grip on the beer bottle.

"Here it comes, baby doll," Peterson said to his helpless victim. "Now you're going to realize that between me and your dead porker husband, I got the bigger gun."

Peterson's moment of fun was suddenly smashed to pieces when a beer bottle somehow flew right through his face. Pieces of glass pierced his right cheek and nose as other fell onto the floor on his right side. The impact of the beer bottle nearly made the horny hunter fell over to his side, which made him release his grip from Olivia's head.

That had given her chance to escape from him and the bar completely. She quickly pulled her jeans back up and ran out of the back door of the bar, nearly stumbling over certain junk that were near the doorway.

"Olivia!" Jessica cried out as she watched the poor red-headed, single mother ran out of the back and into the dark rainstorm.

Olivia ran and ran and ran. The rain soaked her entire body from head to toe and with the enormous amount of drops falling in front of her; she could not see where she was going. Hell, her sense of direction was mulled by the whole experience that all she wanted to do was to run. Run away from her pain, run away from her anguish and run away from her sadness.

She fell on the sidewalk which was filled with a river of rainwater. She laid there for a good while as the rain drops kept banging on her back, soaking her t-shirt like as if it was nothing. She could not take it anymore. She just wanted to die in the street, either by her own pain or drowned by the constant rainwater.

Something flashed into her mind. There was a child, no, not just a child. Little Jake Miller, standing out in the backyard of their house with a smile holding something in his hand to what it appeared to be a small frog.

Further down the yard was a tall man standing, talking to one of the neighbours. It was Jeremy, Olivia's husband and Jake's father talking to Derek Craig, Alan and Alice's father. That was the time when Jeremy came down to Greensburg from Carlton City to visit his family for the first time. They were both happy together as a family and remembering that time had made Olivia smile under the cold, wet rain.

The vision then shifted to another time period, later after Jeremy's funeral. Jake was playing in the backyard along with his new neighbouring friends Alan and Alice. All three of them were playing hide and seek and a few games of tag. There was one time they were playing Cowboys and Indians in which Alan acted out as the cowboy, with a toy revolver, cowboy hat and even a badge. Jake played as an Indian with his hand-made bow and arrow, wearing a bandanna with a black crow's feather on his head and Alice was the damsel in distress held captive by the Indian.

Seeing those two memories in Olivia's mind had made her wonder about her current situation and it suddenly became clear. She may had lost her job at the diner, she may had huge amounts of financial debts, and she may had lost a caring husband who may need to work on his priorities a little, but all she did not lose the most was what she had loved and cared for so long, her own son Jake. And with that in her mind, she finally got up from the pool of rainwater mixed with soot, dirt and particles of the sidewalk, and finally headed for home.

Olivia arrived home, soaked and tempered by the rain. Normally she would hang her purse on a hook somewhere, but she had already realized that she had left it at the Jessica's tavern.

Tired from all the running and possibly going to catch a cold, Olivia decided to sat down at the nearby dining table and relax for a bit before going to bed.

"Mommy," a child's voice ran through Olivia's ears.

She slowly turned her tired head to the three-foot-tall standing at the bottom of the stairs with his little pyjamas on.

"Jake," Olivia said to her son. "You should be in bed, honey. It's very late."

Jake just stood there, wanting to say something but he did not want to anger his mother for what he had to say.

"I want to go back," Jake said softly.

"Go back," Olivia said curiously, "go back to what?"

"I want to go back to the city."

Olivia could not believe what she was hearing. Going back to Carlton City? That's just crazy.

"Honey," Olivia said as she got up from her chair and walked to her child. "We can't go back there. That city is too dangerous, even for both of us."

"It wasn't so bad with dad around."

Olivia wished she hadn't heard that. She had a very good reason to move out of the city with Jake to Greensburg. The city had the highest crime rate in Canada, even more so than USA's New York and Los Angeles combined.

"Jake," Olivia's voice was getting a little sincere. "We had to move out of there because of all the bad things that's happening there."

"Then why didn't dad move in with us?"

"Jake, he had to stay there because of his job."

Olivia was already getting tired with the conversation and just wanted to go to bed and Jake looked like he was getting angry with every answer to his questions.

"I want to go back to where things were." Jake's voice rose.

"Me too, Jake," Olivia's voice raised a bit higher than her son. "But we can't. We can't afford to go back. And even if we could afford it, what difference will it make? Now, go back to bed. We'll talk about this tomorrow."

"No!" Jake suddenly yelled. "I want to go back now."

"Jake! Don't argue with me with this. If we can't do it, we can't do it, period."

"This is all your fault, mom."

Olivia's eyes widened with shock about what she had heard from her own son.

"This is all happening since we moved here. When we were with Dad, we were okay. Daddy was always there to protect us from the bad people. You were just scared."

Olivia kneeled down toward Jake.

"I was scared for you, sweetie!" Olivia said.

She tried to calm the child down with some of her motherly love but it didn't seem to work. Tears were already rolling down Jake's round cheeks. He missed his father so much that we wished he would go back in time to where they were all together, happy and full of life, despite the horrendous crimes and corruption that infested Carlton City.

"I want Daddy back!" Jake cried. "You bring him back, mom!"

"Jake, I..."

"It's all your fault, mom. You didn't love him, that's why we moved. It's your fault he's not here! It's your fault that he's dead!"

And at that moment, Jake felt a hard slap across his left cheek. The sound was loud and almost echoed around the room. Jake felt hurt but not by the slap on the face by his mother but the inside of his lower lip was slightly torn by his lower teeth, tearing into the flash by the impact of the slap. It was enough for it to even bleed out of his mouth.

Olivia saw the blood dripping from her son's mouth. Seeing that made her realized what she had just done and by impulse rather than thinking about it. Her action had caused her six-year-old son to bleed and she stood there, shocked at what she had done.

"Why did you do that, mom?" Jake cried even louder. "Why did you hit me like that?"

Olivia tried to answer, at least trying to apologize, but she could not speak any words that may fix the mistake she had just caused.

"Why did you hit me?" Jake cried again. "I hate you! I hate you, and I wish you were dead!"

Jake ran up the stairs and into his bedroom as Olivia just stood there like a frozen statue. The damage was done, and there was nothing she could do to fix it, not even making up for it. Thinking that everything would turn out okay after losing one job, and then it suddenly gotten even worse than what you would expect. Hearing those three words after she had impulsively slapped his son like that made her heart break even more than before. She too wanted to return things the way it was, when the whole family was together.

Olivia's mind was blank but filled with great emotional pain. She cried but quietly and inside her own soul. She was at turning point to where she would decide to continue on like this, or maybe, probably, decide to end it. And that decision was made when she walked back out into the rain and into the storage shed in the back.

Jake had cried himself to sleep. The bleeding from his mouth had stopped and had already stained his white pillows. He was dreaming of fond memories with his mom and dad when they were all living in the city. The playing, laughing, and joy that they had shared as a family.

Olivia peeked into Jake's room, staring at the sleeping child with his cheeks still wet from his tears. But Olivia's tears kept rolling down hers as she tried not to make a sound. Her thoughts went back and forth, reminiscing the time she and Jake had spent together and the times she and her late husband had shared.

But with an old piece of yellow rope held into her hand, she wanted to say goodbye to her loving son, and hoping that her sister Laura, Jake's aunt would take care of him in the future. But before walked away toward her bedroom, she was able to say two words, two times in succession.

"I'm sorry. I'm sorry."

Chapter 11

I'M sorry, I'm sorry. Those were the exact words he had heard from that demonic creature that wore Jake's mother's face when it came after him. It became clear that Jake's hidden sin was he betrayed his own mother and she even took the blame for it which drove her to suicide. All the wonderful times that he and his parents had spent together and his mother had to make a decision, for her son's sake.

No, Jake thought as tears started running down his cheeks. It is not Mom's fault. It shouldn't have been her fault. It turned out that it was his fault that her mother killed herself that night, all because he was so proud of his father and wished that everything would be back to normal, when the whole family would be together.

But no, Jake had said those harsh words to his own mother. He cannot deny that fact. And now he wished that he could die for the terrible sin of betraying his mother like that because of his father. She cared for Jake, raised him, being by his side when he was sick in bed or in pain from falling. His mother had loved her all those years and ten years ago, her own son had killed her.

"I'm the one who should be sorry, Mom," Jake spoke to himself while staring at the old ceiling lamp to where the old yellow was tied to ten years ago that held her mother in the air. "I'm the one who should be apologizing for saying those words. And I wish that I can see you one more time so that I can beg you for your forgiveness. I'm sorry, Mom. I'm really, truly sorry."

Jake went down on his knees, digging into the dusty, wooden floor of his mother's bedroom. He was feeling terrible and wished that he could just let his own guilt rot inside and kill him in the process. He cried for nearly an hour, feeling the terrible anguish of the terrible sin he had committed. If that shadow creature would come back for him again, Jake would let him and if he were to die by this creature, then so be it. He would rather die than to be continually tortured by his own suffering.

Jake's watery eyes caught his attention of something in the room. An old wooden desk stood several feet away from the old bed frame with a small desk lamp. Covered in layers of dust and mould, the desk was used by Jake's mother for when she would sometimes sit down and write in her diary. The flimsy-looking old chair was even older than the house itself as it was given to her by one her neighbours when she and Jake had finally settled into their new home.

Jake had remembered the times when he would go see his mother sitting at her desk at night or sitting in her bed reading her favourite book. Of course, she wouldn't let him read his diary since her entries were her personal thoughts and liked to keep them hidden for in case she would grow old and not remember anything.

Jake looked around the desk for a while, passing his fingers around the surface. If the diary would still be in the house, then it must be hidden in some secret compartment, or a small chest full of photos, or something. But as Jake's hands went under the desk, his fingers had felt something. His fingers had touched straight cracks that seemed to go around with sharp corners with every turn. It felt like something squared. And as Jake's middle touched the middle of the square, his finger was somehow able to push it upward like a button or some kind of latch.

It made a tumbling sound in one of the right side. Jake slid open the bottom drawer and noticed that the bottom panel came loose. After removing the panel, he a long and squared peg in which his finger had pushed and next to it was a large dark book with the name 'Olivia Chambers' on the hard, front cover.

And there it was his mother's diary, still in good condition aside from all the dust and cobwebs it had collected. This was probably what the stranger had meant. But why would he want his mother's diary? What could a journal full of Olivia's personal thoughts and feelings have that would be so important? Or even a better question, how?

Jake wanted to find out for himself so opened his mother's personal journal. Several entries she had written were somehow faded and illegible while others seemed to clear enough to read. Pages and pages of thoughts and feelings, each of them indicate the date she had written them. She had written down an entry every night, detailing from how she felt when she woke up to seeing certain things that was going on to how school had been doing with Jake.

Jake decided to fine the last diary entry that his mother had written before her death. After several flips of pages, he had found one that was date ten years ago. The date and month was also indicated along with the year, in which Jake remembered that day all too well.

Without any hesitation and wiping the left over tears from his face with the sleeve of his jacket, he began to read his mother's last diary entry.

Alan walked into the church. The interior was dark, dreary and not a single light was shown, not even a candle. Alice said that she would be at the church but having no lights in the area at all could mean that it was recently deserted.

"Alice?" Alan called out but there was no reply. Only echoes of his own voice rang through the walls and pillars of the church.

"Pastor Mayne?" Alan called out again, but there were still no answer.

Where they could have gone, Alan thought. Only thing he could do at the moment was give Alice a call.

'*I'm sorry,*' an automatic voice spoke in to Alan's ear. '*The number you've dialled cannot be reached*'

"What the fuck is going on?" Alan nearly shouted and nearly threw his cell phone on the wooden floor.

Alan took out his flashlight and scanned the darkened interior of the church briefly before trying to call Alice again. But he gotten madder and more worried about his little sister as the same automatic voice repeated the same message.

He tried sending a text message, but he knew that if Alice wouldn't answer her cell, she probably would not receive his message.

"Come on, Alice," Alan spoke to himself, fidgeting a little. "If you were going to see Pastor Mayne but the church is completely empty, where else would you find him?"

The answer struck him obviously and cursed at himself for being that stupid. "You'd be at Mayne's house and he's most likely there at this time of night. Why the fuck didn't I think of that?"

Alan turned around and exited the empty church with much haste. Mayne house was located further down the street on the same side as the local tavern. Passing by several houses, his thoughts were on Alice and hoping she would be alright. Having no answer from her cell and no reply from his text message could mean that her cell phone may have been turned off.

But knowing Alice, she wouldn't turn her phone off unless she's in bed or in the shower. She would use it to text random messages to her friends and sometimes talk to them on hours end on several gossips. And Alan had hoped that she would continue doing that.

Alan's cell phone rang. He stopped walking and looked at the little LCD screen to see who as calling. Alice's name was written on it and Alan did not hesitate to answer it.

"Alice," Alan spoke into his cell phone. "Are you okay? What happened?"

There was dead air, but Alan could almost hear some noise in the background, like a muffled voice. It quickly gotten louder and Alan's heart began to race even more as he recognized the muffled girl's voice he heard through the earphone of his cell.

"Alice," Alan spoke loudly. "Is anybody there with you? Where's Mayne?"

Alice's muffled voice disappeared, but then, a sound of heavy breathing was audible.

"Thou believe in God?" A sharp, eerie whisper seeped into Alan's ear as if it was close by.

"Who the fuck is this," Alan said madly. "What did you do to Alice? Is that you, Mayne?"

"If thou believe in the Father, and the Son, and the Holy Spirit, then join thy sibling at the house of this old man, for he too is among us."

Alan nodded. "When I find you, I'm going to shove The Holy Bible up your ass before I place you under arrest for kidnapping!"

"Then come join us, if thou believe."

The whispering stranger hung up.

"Fuck this!"

Alan picked up the pace, going for Mayne's house.

As soon he arrived there, he noticed the front door was slightly ajar and there were no signs of any light. Alan knew that he may walk right into a trap but he would rather see his little sister alive than saving his own neck. He removed the 9mm from his belt holster, removed the safety lock readied it like he was trained.

The young deputy turned on his flashlight and began scanning the inside of the house. Just like the church, the place looked deserted.

"Alice?" Alan called out. "Pastor Mayne?" And just like at the church, there was no reply. "Is anybody here?

Alan kept going further and carefully with his gun firmly at the ready. Aiming at every turn and every corner he saw, he was hoping that he would find that creepy bastard, but more hopingly to find his sister unharmed.

He heard a noise from upstairs. It sounded like a tumbling noise or the sound of moving furniture. Alice and Mayne had got to be up there without any doubt. But Alan decided not to rush upstairs to find out as there was a high possibility that the stranger who was holding them hostage might there, waiting for him.

As soon as he got upstairs, Alan carefully checked the dusty old study. With a scan of his flashlight, there was no one there. He then went into what appeared to be a guest room. The same, he had found nothing.

There was another sound but closer. It was the same muffled sound of Alice's voice as what he heard over the phone. Hearing that almost made Alan rush into the next room, in which where the sound was coming from.

Upon entering the room and scanned it around with his flashlight, he finally spotted Alice tied up to a chair with an unconscious Brain Mayne tied behind her.

Alan was glad that his sister was still alive and not hurt. He quickly approached the two hostages and attempting to untie them both.

"You okay, Alice?" Alan asked.

Alice replied with a nod, since she could not speak due to having a large towel wrapping around her head, gagging her mouth from ever speaking.

With a quick glance, Alan noticed that Pastor Mayne was bleeding from his bald head, a possible indication that he got hit by a blunt object. Alice was very fortunate to not have any injuries on her.

"Is that guy around?" Alan asked as he was having a difficult time untying the knot.

Alice nodded again.

With that answer, Alan reached for his radio.

"This is Deputy Alan Craig," he spoke in, "I need some units at Brian Mayne's estate. Suspect holding two people hostages. I'm setting them free, now. Suspect possibly armed and dangerous."

Alan's radio replied to his call.

But Alice's eyes had suddenly caught the attention of something approaching her brother behind him. All she could see was yellow glowing eyes and was wearing dark, circular hat, similar to what the Amish would wear. And seeing a white square on his collar indicated that this dark figure was a priest, like Brian Mayne.

Alice tried to signal Alan to look behind him, but he should have removed the gag first before attempting to untie her and the old priest.

Alan noticed Alice's signal and quickly looked behind him, but it was too late. Alice may have seen the dark priest, but Alan only saw a wooden baseball bat flying into his face.

Jake's eyes followed the curvy words of his mother's handwriting. Her last diary entry had depicted bad events that happened during the day, including how she had lost her job at the local diner due to her depression and mental fatigue. It then followed by the time when she worked at the local bar and what had happened with Old Man Peterson.

He remembered when Peterson was in the cell and how he said to Jake that he could have been his new dad. That made Jake even more madder than that time he told him that. He would deserve more than just a solid punch in the face. But dying of a heart attack while he was in his jail cell had sounded more subtle.

Jake kept on reading until he came across a couple of lines that disturbed him a little. But after reading over and over again, his breathing suddenly stopped, his heart felt like stalling and his whole body froze to the reaction of what he had read. And at the time, he wished that he hadn't read it. Even better, he wished he hadn't found the diary in the first place.

'Dear Diary,

I'm not sure if I can describe what had happened to me, today. To begin with, God had picked a lousy day for me to lose my job at the local diner. It rained so badly all day and night and my car decided to stall before picking up Jake after school.

Luckily, Derek happened to drove by and towed my car along the way. He was generous enough to even have my brought to his place to get it fixed at no cost at all. And Jake stayed over at his place for the rest of the afternoon with Alan helping him with his homework.

I have never been so tired and weary in all my life. Because of Jeremy's death and left this world with so much financial debt that working two jobs is too much for me. But having to lose one not only hampered my chances of clearing any debt, but at it least gave me some time to relax and spend some time with Jake.

But at the local bar, Chad Peterson and his friends had to show up. And just like every weekend, whenever it's hunting season, they would drink like as if they were never satisfied. But when I was about to clean up one empty table, Peterson tried to have his way with me. Jessica tried to help out but Peterson's gang of drunks were holding her, giving Peterson the time he wants to...enjoy me.

The first thought of it was seeing my husband Jeremy stepping right in and smack Peterson down of the floor. But my husband is dead, and all the other customers just sat there watching like uncaring owls. I tried to break free but Peterson was too strong for me.

Then he tried to make his way inside me. That was even worse than the dancing we had done. I tried calling for help, yelling and screaming but it was no use. But I was lucky to have an empty bottle and used it on that fucker Peterson, which gave me the opportunity to escape and run out of the bar

I finally arrived home, soaking wet due to the rainstorm. After a moment of rest, Jake came downstairs with an upset look on his face. He wanted to go back, back to Carlton City. Why? Why in God's name does he want to back to that awful city? The real reason he and I moved to Greensburg is to have Jake growing up in peaceful and safe environment, opposed to the violence and the garbage of the city streets.

We both had an argument and Jake tried to win. Hearing him saying that it was my own fault that we didn't bring his father was very hurtful. It wasn't my fault to begin with. If it wasn't for Jeremy and his stupid job at the city's police department, we wouldn't be in this mess. And to make's matters worse, he blamed me for his father's death.

Hearing that, I could not control what happened next. I slapped my own son hard enough just to make him stop saying those words, but it just made things even more worse for me. First, he was bleeding, in which it wasn't my intention to do. Then, he cried so hard that to even say that he hates me, and wished I was dead too.

Normally, a child at such a young age would say those things and never meant it. But that's kind of difficult for me, since I could not share the intensity of love and care to a child as a real mother would do.'

"Like a real mother?" Jake repeated those words to himself, confused by the meaning. He continued reading the entry.

'This is the hardest entry I have ever written, as it feels like it may be my last. Months after Jeremy's death, everything was going downhill for me. I prayed and prayed for any sort of miracle that helps me escape from this torment. But the only answer I was given was the hatred of my adopted son who missed his father way too much.'

"Adopted son," Jake repeated, getting more and more confused. "What the hell…"

'But Jeremy and I had promised to take this secret about Jake to our graves. Who knows, those awful people might still be looking for him, since we stole him away from them when he was still a newborn. I even told my sister Laura if that in anything happens, she would look after our little Jake for the time being.

And I'm pretty sure that Jake will find out as he grows up, his adoption, the people searching for him, The Order of the Holy Light, everything. But I could not imagine how he would feel if he finds out that his father and I are not his biological parents.

I will leave this final entry and hid this diary in the secret compartment underneath the desk drawers. I'm pretty sure someone will find it and give this to Jake. All I can say is that I cannot carry on like this anymore and the only way out for me is to liberate my soul from this broken shell. As for Jake, I have loved him as if he was my own and I will always love him when I pass on to the other side.

And if Jake were to find this diary and read this last entry, all I can say to you, is that I'm sorry. I'm very sorry. I hope you can find some way to forgive me.

Goodbye, Diary. Goodbye, Greensburg. Goodbye, Jake.

Chapter 12

THE shadowed priest dragged Alan's unconscious body to the side. His face was concealed in darkness, like a blanket that hid his true features from the light. His yellow eyes were full and glowed like the eyes of panther. He could see in the dark. His yellow eyes acted like a pair of small flashlights that seemed to be emitted from his very soul.

The figure of this stranger was tall, almost thick but slim at the same time. His clothes were of priest, dark blending easily with the darkness around the room where his captives were held.

He did not looked human, as Alice looked into the bright yellow eyes of the dark priest, similar to what she saw when that shadow demon took her boyfriend away. And when he spoke, it sounded scratchy but most likely loud whispers. And his accent was almost old and ancient, using old dialects when it came to referring to someone.

"Thou did thy best, Brother Mayne," the shadowed priest said to the semi-unconscious old man. "But The Order of the Holy Light requires thy relic to achieve greatness."

The dark priest yanked Mayne's medallion from his neck. He then was able to remove the crucifix from the old relic that was given by Mayne's father.

"Thou faith is strong," the shadowed figure continued, "but thou art too foolish to even think that thou shall find salvation from the Almighty. But we brothers of the Holy Light will bring the ultimate salvation on this world that God had created, and corrupted by sins of Man. The boy that was stolen from us will bring the shadows of salvation to Earth by swallowing it whole, removing it from sin, and we will start anew as we create Heaven on Earth."

The shadowed priest picked up a canister of gasoline that he had brought and started spilling it around the room. Alice knew what the stranger was going to do and she struggled to set herself free before this inhuman stranger set the whole house on fire.

"Within the darkness," the shadowed priest said as he flicked an old Zippo lighter, "let there be light. When there is a greater cause, let there be sacrifices."

And with those cryptic words, the shadowed priest released the Zippo lighter. The miniature flame touched the flammable liquid in front of him as it engulfed into larger flames. The fire was spreading quickly and savagely around Alice, Mayne and Alan as the dark stranger walked out of the room to pour some more gasoline downstairs.

Alice tried to struggle free from the binding rope between her and Pastor Mayne. What worried her more was Alan not waking up. His nose was broken, bleeding constantly all over the wooden floor. The impact the dark priest had delivered was enough to knock her brother out for a while, making her unaware of ravaging fire that was quickly approaching.

Pastor Mayne was sort of in and out of it. He did cough a few times due to the smoke, but his consciousness was barely there. Moaning and groaning from time to time, as his mind tried to repair itself from the damage the shadowed stranger had done to him.

Alice kept on struggling to set free and hoping that Alan would wake up soon before the fire could take their lives. But she can't scream for help since she was still gagged. She had to find a way to get free, but all she could do was keep struggling to set free and pray for any help would arrive.

Jake froze in shock after reading his mother's last words, nearly dropping the diary on the floor. Some of the handwritten words kept repeating in his head like a hidden voice, tormenting him about the truth. He could not believe it; he didn't want to believe it. But his mother's last words before she took her life were genuine, real, and above all, true.

It was all a lie, Jake thought. Sixteen years living in this world and turned out to be a lie. The happy moments of his childhood, his mother, his father, friends and relatives were not his to begin with. They were all fakes, actors, pretenders, playing with his mind and feelings as if it were all real.

Jake fell to his knees. Flabbergasted, shocked, and confused, he just wanted to erase the truth.

"It's not true," Jake whispered to himself. "I won't believe that it's true. But if these were my mom's real thoughts, then why didn't she tell me? Why didn't my own aunt tell me?"

Jake shook his head angrily. "No, she's not my aunt. I'm not related to her, not related to Becky. My mother is not my real mother so I can't be related to them."

And then, Jake's father came into mind. How he was a police detective, a protector of his own family. How Jake looked up to him like a real hero, the type you don't find in comic books or on TV. He was proud of his father and he even dreamed of being a detective just like him. But everything changed after his death, in which had made Jake's dreams shot down like those gangs that attacked the store in which his father was while on his way to see his own family.

Though it was true that Jake had wished everything would go back to normal, when they were living in Carlton City together as a family. But if only his father, Detective Jeremy Miller, had moved with to Greensburg with them, they would still be happy and both parents would be very proud of seeing their own son graduating from Greenburg High School.

But even if that were so, there was no denying the fact that Jake was an adopted child. Jeremy and Olivia Miller had stolen a child from a group of people and had been trying to raise him as their own, hiding Jake's true identity from this so-called 'The Order of the Holy Light.'

It didn't matter; his whole life was still a fake. He didn't have parents to begin with. All of what he had were just props and toys just to make his life a stage-play. And with this shadow creature that stalking him all this time, waiting for its chance to nab him from this cruel world, there was nothing for him to turn back to.

Jake suddenly felt a chill around him, a coldness that he was all too familiar with. But the only light source around to have his own shadow visible would be his own flashlight. That meant that the creature may be somewhere around him, possibly surrounding him. He sat there on his knees, digging into the wooden floor and waited, waited for the thing to take him away from the awful truth, and his fabricated life.

"Take me," Jake said to the surrounding darkness. "I may have committed a sin by betraying my mother, but it turned out she wasn't really my mother. So I guess that means my sin is actually living an entire life full of lies. I have nothing, in this world. Please, take me and get it over with. I have nothing in this life."

The shadows closed in on him like a pool of crude oil, flooding the room with its darkness and death.

"Like Hell, you do!" a male voice cried out from nowhere.

Jake then opened his eyes quickly and saw a flaming bottle flying passed him like a fire ball. The bottle crashed into a portion of the darkness in front of him, spreading the flames across the surface underneath the desk.

Shrieks and distorted cries ringed loudly as another bottle of Molotov crashed onto the floor on Jake's left side.

"Come, on Jake!" the voice shouted. "Let's get out of here!"

Jake looked back to where the voice was coming from. It was that man he saw at the hospital, wearing the same trench coat and dark glasses. The same stranger Jake spotted at the Greensburg cemetery.

"This way!" the man shouted again.

Jake quickly got up before the fires the man had cause nearly got close to him. They both quickly ran down the stairs as the man opened his jacket, grabbed another bottle of Molotov from in the inside pocket, lit the handkerchief that was dangling out from the mouth, lit it up with a lighter and threw it at the living room.

The fire had spread all over the old house. Both Jake and the stranger watched it from outside as they could barely hear the shrieks and cries from the shadow creature, writhing in pain by the burning light of destruction.

Alice kept struggling to set free as the flames were getting closer. She kept on trying to yell for her unconscious brother but her voice was still gagged. She then tried pushing the gag downward onto her chin with her tongue in which she was able to do so. She was then able to breathe but only to have some stolen by the smoke of the roaring fire surrounding her and the two unconscious men.

Alice looked toward Alan, still lying on the floor unconscious with a bleeding nose.

"Alan!" Alice cried out, but there was no response. Alan was completely out of it. "For God's sake get up!"

Tears began running down from her eyes, passing several beads of sweat from the burning heat. She would not want her brother to be smothered by the flames. Not when he just regained his role as an officer of the Greensburg Police Department. And losing a brother like that would be even more painful for her than having their mother being wasted away by Carlton City's corruption. She would pray to God and hoping to get some kind of answer, some kind of sign that would help them. But the fire was spreading too quickly, maybe even quicker than whatever message that God would send to three of His children who were about to be burned alive.

A portion of the flames was nearing Alan toward his feet. Alice kept on trying to set free as quickly as she could before the flames actually touch her only brother, but the dark priest had bounded her and Pastor Mayne very tightly. "Alan. Wake up, damn it!" Alice cried louder as the tongues of the fire suddenly lit up one of Alan's shoe laces.

"ALAN!"

"TOO bad," the stranger said having a nostalgic feeling, "your mother loved that house. I personally found it cosier than the one we were before, back at the city."

"Is it dead?" Jake asked, still watching the flames burning his old home away.

The man shook his head. "No, it probably went back to wherever it came from. Did you get the diary?"

Jake didn't answer but pointed at the burning house.

"Oh well," the man nearly raised his shoulders. "It's probably for the best."

Jake turned his attention to the stranger as the stranger returned the favour. As soon as the middle-aged man took off his dark glasses, Jake's both his breathing and his heart had stopped in an instant. He had recognized the man's face all too well. He remembered it from his own childhood, despite being a total fabrication. He remembered the phone call his mother had received about the terrible news, and the funeral that followed after.

Jake just stood there, frozen as if he had seen a ghost. He knew who the stranger was and he knew his name. But he was too shocked to talk in plain conversation, so he was able to say only one word.

"Dad?"

To Be Continued...

THE DEVIL WITHIN
-Awakening the Beast-

FIRST CHAPTER PREVIEW

NOTE: *This preview is considered as the first draft and does not represent the final version. Names of people and places may differ upon final release*

-1-

THE CITY LIT UP LIKE A CHRISTMAS TREE. Every square feet, every kilometre, almost every building had shown some light emitting from their windows and streets. With every ounce of Heaven's light, it gave the citizens some form of sanctuary from the dreary darkness that engulfs the sky. Of course from a distance, seeing the city lights would look beautiful. But between the buildings and the people walking up and down the streets, the dark shadows within the damp alleys were home of the worst kind of people from different forms of life.

Murderers, rapists, pickpockets, muggers and even druggies lived among the innocent and the faithful. The corrupting society that spread across the city like a virus and not even one living soul is safe from those foul excuses of humankind. Everywhere you would look, every turn of your head, and every corner of your eye, you would see them. Either they be pumping themselves with narcotics or having their way with some helpless victim who had not yet finished high school.

That is exactly what was going through Dustin Gale's mind as he walked down the streets from his visit of his family doctor. From every glance toward every direction, he would notice elements of the city's corruption. Street punks harassing the innocent, vehicles getting broken in and valuables taken, even a small few would even steal a vehicle as their ticket out of the city from the police chasing them. Even though his father was an officer of the law, he had little faith in justice as well as the system itself. He had pretty much lost it when his father was killed by a random street gang and the police force were too scared to even lay a finger on those responsible due to lack of resources and some possible influence to some of the city's population.

Dustin's kept on walking gazing into his mind, hoping to find some kind of resolve. But his inner-concentration was suddenly interrupted when his entire body felt like it walked into wall. No, not a wall, but a tall, large person. The red spiky hair, three piercing on each of his ears and a tattoo of a cracked skull was barely seen behind the black tank top on his back. Just seeing all those features, Dustin immediately knew that whoever he bumped into was not friendly, nor an innocent bystander.

"Watch where you going, you fucking retard," the spiky-haired punk shouted. "Are you fucking blind or something?"

Dustin tried not to look into the punk's eyes as they looked menacing enough to make even the bravest of men quiver in their boots.

"I'm so sorry," Dustin stuttered a little. "I'll be more careful next time."

Dustin tried to walk pass the menacing street punk, but only to bump into another one like him. Except this one was more muscular, looked even stronger enough to probably even break the bones of the other.

"Apologizing isn't good enough," the bald-headed muscle man barked. "You'll need to pay up in order to pass us."

Dustin was getting more afraid than ever, since he did not have any cash, nor any change, to pay the two punks.

"Well," a scratchy, female voice echoed nearby. "By the looks of this kid, maybe he can pass up his virginity."

A skinny, skank-looking, woman walked up to the scene. She was wearing a short, pink vest over her barely see-through tank top with dirty-looking furs around the collar, due to her chain smoking. Her fishnet stockings had a few wider gaps but it wasn't enough to cover her freckled, bony legs. She looked like a drunken, full-baked prostitute with insatiable hunger for one-night stands.

Dustin could not find a way to escape the predicament. The only way out was to give them something, but unfortunately, he had nothing of value. And because of that, the only way out was to lose some of his dignity, or maybe his life.

The spiky-haired punk snatched Dustin's coat yanked him fiercely toward his decorated face. The punk's nose had a golden ring through his left nostril and three metal stubs were visible on each of his eyebrows.

"You better give me something quick," the spiked-haired punk barked as small spittle flew at Dustin's face, "or I will give you a fucking face lift."

Dustin was trembling. His own heartbeat was so loud and painful that he could hear it. Every beat he heard made him imagine the impact of the punk's fists if they were to connect with his seventeen-year-old face. But after a few moments, that plan was interrupted.

Dustin felt a throbbing pain in his heart, as if it was pushing really hard to pump more blood while it kept beating like a drum. He clutched his chest with his right hand, hoping that it won't burst out. With his left hand, he searched in his jacket pocket for a little bottle of pills that had gotten from his family doctor.

Seeing what was going on with Dustin, the spiky-haired punk was curious with his victim's sudden reaction but then quickly made a smirk as if the whole thing was amusing to him.

"What the fuck's wrong with you?" he laughed. "Getting a heart attack at your age, or something?"

The punk tossed Dustin aside like a helpless rag doll. The impact of the fall made Dustin's pill bottle flew out of his jacket pocket and rolled several inches away. Dustin tried to hurry toward the bottle before he would lose it, but the pain so unbearable that he had a hard time crawling toward his only thing that would save him.

"Let's go, guys," the spiky-haired punk said to his two subordinates. "This weakling is a waste of time."

Dustin was able to obtain the pill bottle. He popped the cap open and swallowed one of the small, red and white capsules before snapping the cap back on. And within half-a-minute, the pain in his heart slowly eased and the fast beating was reducing to normal. Though while waiting for everything to return to normal, he did over heard of what that spiky-haired punk had said and that made him little more upset than his abnormal heart condition.

According to what his family doctor had told him, Dustin Gale was born with an unknown heart condition. It seemed kind of normal at first glance, but that particular muscle that pumps blood back and forth through his veins and arteries was very sensitive to certain situations the seventeen-year-old student of Bastion High School would come across. Whenever he would get to excited, nervous, or even when he would do something that requires a lot of physical activity, including running or jumping, his heart rate would jump five times more than an average human would bear. And with so much pumping involved, Dustin's doctor was getting concerned about the heart's physical integrity. Too much pumping or even excess of it may cause his heart to rupture at any given time.

After figuring the diagnosis, Dustin's doctor prescribed him with some form of medication which involved capsules filled with two powdered drugs. The white half was supposed to provide some sort on pain reliever while the red one was supposed to be something to keep his heart beat regulated. It all sounded too complicated for Dustin, but after ingesting one of those capsules, it turned out to be the real deal.

But having this type of medication and the condition he was born with, the doctor had told him he would not be able to do any type of fun, physical activity such as playing basketball without risking his own heart to be ruptured inside his chest. He even told him not to be too stressed at any given time and avoid anything that might cause his heart to go out of control. But in order for him keep him relaxed and calm; he would have to drink some kind of chamomile tea or some kind of herbal relaxant. Hearing what the doctor had said about no physical activity like playing basketball had crushed his ultimate dream of being a professional player. Though the only physical activity he could do was walking at his own pace the imagination of running down the courtyard, dribbling with the ball toward the suspended basket and deliver the winning dunk had never ceased from Dustin's mind.

Dustin got himself up from the ground with an upset, angry feeling in his soul. After hearing the word 'weakling' by that street delinquent, it almost made him believing the punk's words. He thought he couldn't do anything, not even defending himself from those poor excuses of humanity. And with that going through his mind, he continued his slow trek for home. Problem was that he was already late and he would expect his mother to be waiting for his son to arrive and give him another scolding for being so late. But what could he possibly do? Would he rather die of a heart rupture out in the street, or being beaten, robbed and left on the sidewalk to die along with his dignity?

About R.J. Levesque

R.J. Levesque has had the interest of writing since the seventh grade. He likes to dwell into the paranormal and supernatural mysteries of storytelling as well as psychological. He is Canadian born in a small town in New Brunswick. He received his school diploma in 2001 from John Caldwell School and currently works for McCain Foods.

R.J. Levesque has been self-publishing for at least a year using Print-On-Demand with his debut novel "The Hidden Sin V1: Lies & Confessions." And you can follow his updates on current and future titles by visiting:

RJLevesqueBooks.Blogspot.com

Facebook.com/R.J. Levesque

Twitter.com/@RikkyL

www.ingramcontent.com/pod-product-compliance
Lightning Source LLC
Chambersburg PA
CBHW030145200626
46812CB00015B/1708